Ted Staunton

Red Deer P R E S S

Published by
Red Deer Press
A Fitzhenry & Whiteside Company
195 Allstate Parkway, Markham, ON L3R 4T8
www.reddeerpress.com

Edited by Peter Carver
Cover design and text design by Tanya Montini
Cover image courtesy Thomas Northcut
Printed and bound in Canada

Financial support provided by the Canada Council, and the Government of Canada through the Book Publishing Industry Development Program (BPIDP).

 Canada Council **Conseil des Arts**
for the Arts **du Canada**

 ONTARIO ARTS COUNCIL
CONSEIL DES ARTS DE L'ONTARIO

Library and Archives Canada Cataloguing in Publication
Staunton, Ted, 1956-
Acting up / Ted Staunton.
ISBN 978-0-88995-441-0
I. Title.
PS8587.T334A67 2010   jC813'.54   C2010-900194-X

Publisher Cataloging-in-Publication Data (U.S)
Staunton, Ted.
Acting up / Ted Staunton.
Red Deer Press imprint.
[196] p. : cm.
ISBN: 978-0-88995-441-0 (pbk.)
1. Family life – Juvenile fiction. 2. Conduct of life – Juvenile fiction. 3. High schools – Juvenile fiction. I. Title.
[Fic] dc22   PZ7.S738Ac 2010

Preserving our environment

Red Deer Press chose to print the pages of this book on recycled paper and saved these resources[2]:

	energy	water	greenhouse gases	solid waste
	14 million BTUs	76,567 L	1,905 kg	557 kg

ANCIENT FOREST™ FRIENDLY

44 trees were saved for our forests

Printed by Webcom Inc. on Legacy Hi-Bulk Natural 100% post-consumer waste.

Mixed Sources
Product group from well-managed forests, controlled sources and recycled wood or fiber

Cert no. SW-COC-002358
www.fsc.org
© 1996 Forest Stewardship Council

[1]Estimates were made using the Environmental Defense Paper Calculator.

I'd like to thank Peter Carver, a friend indeed,
for wise and witty editorial advice, patience with acronyms
and computerized quotation marks, and faith in this book.

To Will, Mark, the other Sam,

and the class of 2006, Port Hope High School

Part One

BABY

Chapter One

"You can't do *that*," Sam Foster said, breaking through the knots of students outside the Little Hope Variety. "I-i-it—" Unexpectedly, he hit a patch of ice and skidded toward the curb like some kind of uncontrollable adolescent urge.

"Why not?" said Larry, a step or two behind. "Girls li—" He broke off as he, too, hit the ice. Luckily there was a bank of frozen slush to stop them both.

"Well, for one thing, it's February," Sam resumed. "You can't serenade someone outside their window if it's closed. Besides, it's too cold out to play guitar. Your fingers will fall off. And if you're not going to sing, how will she know it's you? *And* how will you know which window is hers? What if you end up pissing off her parents instead?"

"Face it, it's *immature*," Darryl summed up from behind. He hit the slush bank, too. "You want to show her you like her, snap her bra strap. It's way more direct." Darryl shivered. He was facing February in surfer shorts, having vowed to wear them all winter. No one could remember why. He did have a hoodie on over his T-shirt, though, which was more than Sam had on up top. Coats, as any fool knew, were only worn around parents.

And parents brought him back to Darryl's comment. Maturity was a big topic for Sam himself these days. Since December, he'd been frantically atoning for a little—well, okay, big—mistake he'd made, trying to get his parents back around to their original plan of leaving him on his own for a couple of days in March Break, while he took his driver training course. Currently this, and even getting his learner's permit, was hanging in the balance.

They stepped over the slush and out into the road without looking. There were never many cars at lunch; drivers knew better. Back inside the clamorous warmth of Hope Springs High School, they hustled up the stairs with the kind of energy you only had on a Friday afternoon. Especially this Friday afternoon. Tomorrow night, ADHD, Sam, Darryl, and Larry's alt-rock trio, was playing in the Musicurve teen-band battle in Toronto. A ton of kids were going, including Sam's girlfriend Martha. There was a definite vibe in the band that this could be a Big Thing. Of course, in a town the size of Hope Springs, anything livelier than Tuesday qualified as a Big Thing.

At the top of the stairs, Larry said, "Well, I'm going to anyway." Being Larry, that was all he said. He walked away, maybe to his locker, maybe off to be a mystery serenader. With Larry, you never knew. "What girl is it, anyway?" Darryl asked. Then, "I wonder why my legs go all blotchy like that in the cold?"

Sam shrugged as he one-handed the combination for his locker. It wasn't the first time for either question. Besides, the bell was going to ring any second, and his daily tide of anxiety had begun to rise. Their next class was always brutal. Still, he managed to get his locker open, binder and textbook out, and the door closed without ever quite looking at—or smelling—the jumble inside. Nothing fell out, either; two and a half years of high school had not been a total waste.

"C'mon," he sighed to Darryl, as the bell rang. They headed for Family Studies.

Chapter Two

Family Studies was supposed to be the kind of class you could be late for, the soothing grade eleven no-brainer you needed when your semester timetable, like Sam's, also included English, History, French, and Statistical Math. It was also supposed to be taught by Mrs. VanVegel, a cream puff who dressed in vivid pant suits and gave extensions before she even heard your excuse. Unfortunately, Mrs. V had slipped on a condom wrapper at the Christmas dance and injured her back. This semester, Family Studies was being taught by Mr. Tegwar.

Mr. Tegwar had taught biology at Hope Springs High for so long that he had taught parents of his current students, Sam's mom among them. Every spring the rumor—or maybe the prayer—circulated that he was going to retire, but it never happened. Stories about him were legion, but really, his nickname said it all: The Teginator. As he reached the biology lab, Sam saw the man looming just inside the door, looking even angrier than usual. Instinctively, Sam crammed his six feet four inches into a Survival Slouch. There was probably no need; the Teginator was busy destroying a kid from the previous class.

"Well, w-where is it and when do you plan to hand it in?"

Red-faced, the girl clutched her binder like a shield and squeaked a reply.

"That's not good enough. Assignments are not done whenever you ..."

As he slipped by, looking down on the man's silver hair, Sam realized again that Mr. Tegwar was actually too short to loom; he was just one of those people so fierce they seemed to anyway. Martha's friend Lotus was another.

Sam sank onto his stool at one of the lab modules. Behind him, Darryl was saying to someone, "We are so going to *rock their worlds* tomorrow." Sam leaned forward, a move that kept him low and out of Darryl's embarrassing conversation. Darryl had a tendency to make up for Larry's silences.

Sam opened his text and pretended to be engrossed. Martha would be in History right now. Family Studies was all that stood between him and the weekend; he didn't want to mess anything up. Various friends slouched or hustled in and found their places. Steve and Amanda sat down in front of him. On the stool next to him, Delft Hoogstratten settled in. "God, I hate it when he shreds someone," she sighed. Sam nodded in agreement.

Delft opened her binder. "It's going to be fun tomorrow night."

"Yeah," Sam said, perking up and playing a quick drum lick on his module top with his index fingers. "Did you get a ride?"

"Larry's parents. They had room for me and Celeste."

"That's great. We'll need all the help we can get."

"Oh, you guys will rock out."

This was reassuring, coming from Delft. She was an excellent singer in all the ways that he, Darryl, and Larry were not.

The bell rang.

"Your attention. Now."

They stopped talking. You had to be extra careful of the Teginator in last period; by then, his fuse was even shorter. The girl had vanished, probably shredded into a little pile that would be swept up by the caretaker. Up front, the Teginator stood behind the lab counter, rocking slightly, the way he always did. He blinked rapidly several times behind his steel-rimmed spectacles, then his lips pursed and he jutted his chin at the class. This deepened the grim lines around his mouth and gave you an extra-good view of his Adam's apple as it bobbed in his ropy neck. He was wearing his usual lame Friday getup of neck-buttoned check shirt and cardigan sweater. Today, though, something was different. He was awkwardly cradling a bundle of blue cloth. It appeared to be—and Sam blinked here to make sure he wasn't hallucinating—a baby.

"This," said Mr. Tegwar, "is—"

He was interrupted by an eerie electronic wail. The Teginator hurriedly extracted something from his pocket, then, clutching the baby in his other hand, something like a football, tilted it face down and fumbled with a fastening. The wailing got louder. Mr. Tegwar fumbled some more, then appeared to push whatever he'd taken from his pocket into the baby's back. The noise stopped. He tipped what Sam now saw was some kind of doll back up toward the class.

"Th-this," Mr. Tegwar repeated, slightly out of breath, "is a Kinder 4000 Infant Simulator. It is intended to give an understanding of the time and attention a ... uh ... small child demands. The simulator is programmed to cry at random for lengths of time from ten seconds to forty minutes, and can only be deactivated by inserting this key into the slot in its back." Mr. Tegwar turned the doll and showed everyone. "If you remove the key too soon"—he pulled; the wailing started again—"a computer chip inside registers response time as well as failure to keep the key in. For thirty percent of your mark, each of you will be required to care for the simulator—the staff call him ... uh ... Bunny"—the Teginator's lips twitched to indicate a smile—"for a period of seventy-two hours, Monday afternoon through Thursday, or Friday through Monday. You will be given a report form with an essay section. I have drawn up a schedule; it cannot be changed. We begin this weekend"—he peered down at his desk—"with Sam Foster."

Chapter Three

"Welcome to your nightmare," Darryl chuckled. Words of comfort were not his specialty. "We still practicing tonight?"

"Yeah, we'd better." Sam rolled his shoulders against the straps of the blue Snuggles carrier. Baby Bunny nestled against his chest like a small bomb, weighing exactly seven pounds, one ounce, the average weight of a newborn infant, according to the ever-precise Mr. Tegwar.

They were at their lockers again. Sam had his coat on, but unzipped, in case the doll started crying. It had done so twice already, to the delight of the other Family Studiers. Words of comfort were not their specialty, either. Now it began again as Sam shrugged on his backpack, shoulder straps over shoulder straps.

"I'm out of here." Darryl beetled off, shoving his ear buds in.

The key hung on a plastic hospital bracelet locked around Sam's wrist. He undid snaps and zippers, fumbled Baby Bunny's infant shirt up, and jammed in the key. The crying, thank God, stopped. Still holding the key in place, he closed his locker, then slouched down the hall and around the corner to Martha's locker, only to remember she'd said she'd be going straight to work at Jimmy's Pizza. He sighed. It didn't matter; he had things to do, too, before the good part of the weekend began—if there was going to be a good part. At the doors, he got his ear buds in, dialed up Radiohead on his mp3 player, then headed for the public library. As part of his maturity drive, Sam was pushing to finish up the forty hours of volunteer work he needed before graduating.

He'd been a reindeer in the Santa Claus parade, walked dogs for the Humane Society, tried to sell mixed nuts for the Yeswecan service club (luckily, his parents bought some), and been the target for the splash pool at a grade school fun night. His current gig was better: shuttling books back and forth for J. Earl Goodenough, Hope Springs' resident celebrity.

J. Earl was a writer and TV commentator with a knack for upsetting almost everyone. Sam had first met the great man as his paper boy, back in grade six. These days, J. Earl, who was getting up there, had a new "work-in-progress," as he grandly put it. He was writing his memoirs while recovering from hip replacement surgery.

Why you needed other people's books to write about your own life was beyond Sam, especially when you could just look yourself up on the Internet, but J. Earl counted every delivery run as one hour on the volunteer tally sheet, so it was a good deal. So good, in fact, that today's run would complete his hours. Not only was he about to be certified more mature, J. Earl was going to pay him five dollars a trip from now on.

The Kinder 4000 stayed quiet when he took the key out a couple of blocks along. The temperature was dropping. He refastened everything with numbed fingers and zipped his coat up to the Snuggles carrier. Warm could be cool when friends weren't around.

He trudged down the long hill to the Four Corners, the heart of downtown Hope Springs, and the streets grew livelier; Friday afternoons were the busiest time of the week. Sam looked for his mom; her store, the Bulging Bin Bulk Food, was down the block. Jimmy's Pizza, where Martha worked, was a half-block the other way.

He turned onto Queen Street. A lady with a toddler was passing. Her gaze locked on the Snuggles, then cut upward to his face. Her expression soured. Sam barely registered it. Something far more interesting was coming up.

The library itself was ahead, across the street, facing the park with its weary-looking Nativity scene. Just before it, came a new store that had opened in time for Christmas. Sam crossed at the Royal Theater. That way, he didn't look like a heat-seeking missile aimed right at the store's sign that read, in what seemed very sophisticated, somehow French-looking letters:

nicely naughty boutique
A Tastefully Titillating
Erotic Emporium

Even better, notices on the lacy-curtained door and window said shoppers had to be eighteen or older. All of which spelled, in sophisto-French lettering, *exciting possibilities.*

Darryl claimed to have glimpsed a stunning blonde in a pink pushup bra through those curtains, but then Darryl had a thing about bras (although, hey, who didn't?), and he'd also claimed that his guitar had been played by Jimi Hendrix. This was because the guy he'd bought it from had said that *he'd* bought it from a guy who said he'd known Jimi Hendrix's cousin. Or something. Still, you never knew.

As he reached the other curb, Sam noticed another woman frowning at him. A couple behind her did the same. He couldn't help but wonder if everyone was reading his dirty mind. Was his tongue hanging out or something? He tilted his head skyward as if absorbed in Deep Thoughts and Serious Music, just another innocent citizen on his way to volunteer work at the library. He strolled, still gazing at the clouds. Radiohead was laying down the shimmering synth vibe that was "Treefingers." The store was coming up next. He glimpsed sophisto-French. *Now.* Without moving his head, he cut his eyes hard left and down to the window. Something round and creamy swayed behind the curtain. His heart skipped a beat. There was a flash of pink and—WHAM, pain seared his shin.

"*AHH!*" cried Sam. An ear bud popped out. Yapping fractured the afternoon.

A voice rasped, "Hey! What's the matter with yez?"

Wincing, Sam hopped backwards and saw that he had slammed into a bundle buggy. Only something was jumping up and down inside it, which made it not a bundle buggy, but a … what? It looked like a miniature playpen on wheels. Inside it, scrabbling against the mesh sides, was a tiny dog in a green plaid coat. Hauling the contraption was an apple doll of a lady in a matching coat and tam. She looked like a granny. She hadn't sounded like one, though, unless her family were Hell's Angels. Still overcome with pain, all Sam could manage was more hopping and another "*AHH*," as music dinned in one ear and the dog shrilled in the other.

Naturally, the Kinder 4000 began to cry.

"Shit," cried Sam. Still hopping, he tugged at fasteners. Metal slipped under his frozen fingers. Everything got louder. Desperately, Sam shook out the other ear bud, yanked down the zipper on the

Snuggler pouch, and pulled Baby Bunny out by its head, slamming the key in to cut it off in mid-wail. "Sorry," he panted. The pain in his shin was subsiding. A tinny trickle of Radiohead mixed with the dog yips.

Biker Granny stared, open-mouthed. Then her jaw snapped shut. "My God," she breathed, "yer sick." She scuttled off up the street, dragging her playpenned pet behind.

Chapter Four

"But ..." Sam called. His numb fingers slipped on the key; Baby Bunny erupted. A jogger did a double take.

Then the door of *Nicely Naughty* opened. A voice called, "Sam! I thought that was you. What in the world are you doing?" It was Mrs. Gernsbach. She and her husband owned the store.

Sam got the key back in and quiet was restored. "It's for school," he groaned. "I have to keep this key in or it cries, but my fingers are too cold."

"Then come on in. You can't handle everything at once."

"Am I, like ... allowed?"

Mrs. Gernsbach smiled. "No shopping, just warming up."

Everyone knew the Gernsbachs (in Hope Springs, everyone knew everyone) but Sam didn't know anyone who'd confessed to being in their store. *Nicely Naughty* had caused a stir; someone had even started a petition to close it down. Ushered in, Sam stared, while trying not to. Around him, wild colors and lacy extravagance hung next to stamp-sized translucence. What *were* those, over by the board games? He swallowed. Board games? And did that say *edible* over there? And what the heck was *that* next to the batteries? Batteries? *Edible?* He swallowed again. Mrs. Gernsbach had been right about warming up. Suddenly the place felt downright hot.

"So, just what is that thing?" asked Mrs. Gernsbach.

For a panicky instant, Sam thought again that his mind was being read. Then he realized she was referring to the Kinder 4000. Sam explained about Family Studies and the conflict with ADHD.

Mrs. Gernsbach knew about bands. Mr. Gernsbach had been in an adult / teen band called Maple Nitro with Sam, his dad, Darryl, Delft, and some others a couple of years back. As she listened, she straightened a rack of flame-red camisoles. A hefty type, she herself wore a shapeless cream sweater and stretch slacks. She was the conservative dresser in her family; people knew Mr. Gernsbach wore women's clothes around the house. They made him look a little like the Queen. Band rehearsals at the Gernsbachs had been quite interesting.

"Well, I hope you work things out," Mrs. Gernsbach said, then, "oh, goodness." Something pink was crumpled in her hand. She smoothed out a tiny set of panties. Sam couldn't help remembering that Martha had once dyed her hair the same color. An image popped into his head. He felt even warmer.

On the plus side, this meant feeling was returning to his hands. He cautiously removed the key: silence. Thankfully, he bundled the doll back into the Snuggler pouch. It was a relief to have something safe to look at.

Mrs. Gernsbach helped with the last fasteners. "There. Right as rain. Just be glad it's this easy. When ours were little, there were plenty of nights with no sleep at all." She led the way to the door.

"Thanks, Mrs. Gernbach."

"No problem, Sam. And break a leg tomorrow, huh?"

"You bet." He stepped back out into the cold.

"Don't be a stranger!" She merrily waved goodbye with the pink fur panties.

Passersby took in the tableau of Sam, Baby Bunny, *Nicely Naughty*, and Mrs. Gernsbach with the panties. Eyes narrowed. Sam shoved his ear buds back in, then half-slouched, half-hightailed it for the library.

Chapter Five

Don't be a stranger. Sam was still sighing over the words as his dad served chili for supper. It was impossible to be a stranger in Hope Springs, and it drove kids crazy. Martha's mom was always saying, "Just because you're downtown, don't think you're anonymous." She was right, too, although with Martha's hair colors, you wouldn't be anonymous in a football stadium.

By the time he'd gotten home, he'd lost track of how many times he'd explained about the Kinder 4000. He'd met the Hell's Angels granny again in the library, where she'd called him a weirdo. Then she'd checked out a book titled *C is for Chainsaw.*

"Friend of yours, Sam?" Mrs. Stephens the librarian had asked.

"It's a long story." Sam had had no desire to tell it. Mrs. Stephens had saved him the trouble. "Whose baby?"

J. Earl Goodenough, typically, had led with, "What the hell is that?"

His hands full, Sam had been knocking on the door with his head as the doll cried.

"For a second there, I thought it was real," J. Earl had gone on, without waiting for an answer. "But you're a little young. I mean, I was out of the blocks fast myself, but still. I'll tell ya, though, there was a time when Goodenough was more than good enough."

"I'll bet." Sam had shivered, and escaped. Conversation with J. Earl generally didn't require a lot of input.

Conversation with Sam's mom, on the other hand, usually required a lot of input. Or rather, concentration, so revealing input could be avoided whenever possible. Now, at the dinner table, she said, "I hear you were in *Nicely Naughty* today."

Sam groaned inwardly. He should have known.

"It was an accident." Baby Bunny started to cry. He reached his keying arm to the doll. It fell silent, gazing back blankly from a highchair Mr. Foster had dug out from the basement, a relic of Sam and his sister Robin's baby days. Currently Robin was at university, studying journalism.

He explained his mishap, highlighting his innocence. His parents seemed amused. Relieved as he was by this, Sam felt it was unjust.

"It's totally unfair. And all these old people keep glaring at me like I'm some kind of pervert. I can't do *anything*."

"Sure you can do things," said Mrs. Foster, who could be maddeningly practical. "You're eating your dinner right now."

"Yeah, right. With one hand." Sam looked along his outstretched arm to the doll. "I can't even walk down the street."

"Hey," said his dad, buttering a chunk of bread, "don't knock it. It got you into Sin City there. What's the store like?"

"I wouldn't know," Sam sidestepped primly. "I was busy."

"Did it ever occur to you," said his mom, "that that's just the point? That this is what it would be like to be a teen parent?"

"But I'm not going to be a teen parent!" Sam cried.

"Darn right. You and Martha had better be far more sensible—and restrained—than that. But it's a well-known fact that teenage boys think about sex once every six minutes."

"Mom! Geez!" If there was a comparable stat for blushing, Sam felt he was exceeding it. This "fact" had come up a number of times since his December trouble. While Sam privately thought the numbers should be more like once every thirty seconds, it still wasn't something he was inclined to discuss.

To change the subject to something more mature, he announced, "I got my forty hours volunteering done today."

He hadn't been expecting a flourish of trumpets or showers of confetti, but he was still startled when his mom said, "Good. Of course, that doesn't mean you just stop volunteering."

That was exactly what Sam thought it meant. He stopped himself from saying so. Instead, privately, he wondered when this maturity stuff would end. *Driving*, he reminded himself. *March Break. Home alone. You can do it.*

"So," Mr. Foster served salad, "what are you doing tonight?"

"We're supposed to practice. Martha's working; she might come over after."

"When are you doing homework this weekend?"

Sam wasn't even going to dignify this with a response. He said instead, "Anyway, how am I going to play tomorrow night? This is a big show for us."

And it was. If ADHD kicked serious butt in its Toronto debut, the band would be invited back. Who knew what might happen then?

"Hon," said Mrs. Foster. "I'll take the ba—I mean the doll, while you're playing."

Sam shook his head. "I already asked. You can't."

"Why not? Isn't that what a responsible parent would do? Get a sitter?"

"Yeah, but we're not allowed. Mr. Tegwar said parenthood isn't something you can choose not to do for a while, and that the assignment was part of the course description." He picked around something soggy and vegetable in the chili and groused on. "I mean, hello? We just started the course and we got into this show last semester! I didn't get to pick the date we play."

"I'll take the baby," Mrs. Foster repeated. "He'll never know."

"Yes, he will. The stupid key is on a bracelet from the hospital. I can't give it to you without cutting it off."

"So we let it cry for a couple of minutes."

"If you let it cry for one minute, the computer chip registers neglect. At two, it's abuse. Three abuses and you fail. Anyway, you never know how long it's going to cry for after you stick the key in." Sam's sense of injustice peaked, along with his vocal range. He moved his hand, which was beginning to go to sleep. The doll howled. He thought of a particularly juicy obscenity and jammed the key back in.

Mrs. Foster frowned and looked again at the doll, this time with a trace of annoyance. "I was beginning to wonder about that." Then, "Don't worry," she said. "We'll think of something."

Mr. Foster, who was the drama teacher at the high school, puffed out a sigh and raised his beer. "I probably shouldn't mention this now, but Teggy said in the staff room that you can program the doll to different behaviors. He chose cranky."

Sam groaned out loud. Baby Bunny, mercifully, said nothing.

Chapter Six

ADHD practice did not go well. Held in the Fosters' low-ceilinged basement, it featured the usual complement of bumped heads and sore backs, since Sam, the drummer, was the only one who played sitting down. Also, judging by the number of howls it cut loose with, Baby Bunny was not a fan of original alt-rock. Working through their twenty-minute set took Sam, Darryl, and Larry an hour and a half, a lot of it taken up by waiting for Sam to remove the key from the doll's back.

"We're dead if this happens tomorrow," said Larry, stooping even further as he took off his bass.

"Can't you get it to cry like crazy, somehow, just before we play?" Darryl rubbed his own back. "You know, like cry itself out for a while? Or give it a beer and put it to sleep?"

"I can't control it," Sam sighed. He did a test pull on the key. The teeth-vibrating wail started again. He jammed the key back in and wondered what he was going to do. This was an important gig.

"You want to come to—" Darryl began, then looked at Baby Bunny. "Oh, I guess you can't."

"Martha said she might be coming over," Sam said. He didn't feel like going anywhere anyway.

When the others had left, Sam put Baby Bunny into the Snuggler and clunked back down to his drum kit. He picked up his sticks and played a tentative lick. The carrier was tight on his shoulders, but it wasn't too bad. He settled into the rhythm for "Radar Gun," a tune they'd be playing tomorrow night. The doll began to cry. Sam grimaced and put down his sticks. This time, the crying lasted only a few minutes. It wasn't until he was pulling the key out that he noticed that another noise had accompanied the crying. In his frustration, his feet had continued to drive the high-hat and the bass drum. Sam was so used to their sound, he hadn't even noticed them.

He stopped. In the silence that followed, he could hear the furnace ticking. He could also hear his mom sigh, "Thank *God*," from upstairs.

Sam ignored the comment. Pioneering musicians were used to criticism. Instead, he pondered the phenomenon of unconscious foot performance. Slowly, he picked up his sticks, then stopped to adjust the carrier, this time leaving one of the fasteners undone. He began to play.

By nine-thirty, Sam was in the den. Drummers were also used to having limits put on home practice. Now he was delving into the finer points of parallel parking as explained in *The Driver's Handbook*. In its own way, it was every bit as engrossing as *The Big Sleep*, an old detective story his dad had passed him. If his maturity streak continued for another week or so, he'd ask to get his learner's permit. Then he could bring up the topic of March Break and staying alone again. Then, paradise ...

Down the hall the doorbell rang; he heard hear his dad answer.

"Sam! Martha's here."

Sam jumped up. He'd wondered if by now Martha might have gone to her friend Lotus's place instead. He got to the door as his dad finished hanging up her coat. Martha, who had the enviable talent of being able to sound adult around adults, even while having blue hair and two piercings (nose and eyebrow), was saying, "Thanks, that sounds really interesting. I'll think about it."

As they headed for the den, she switched back to normal speech. "Work sucked. God, it was so hot in there."

This reminded Sam of *Nicely Naughty*. He changed the subject. "How come you're not at Lotus's?"

"Grounded," Martha snorted. "She got nailed scoffing out of her mom's purse."

Sam applauded inwardly. He didn't much care for Lotus and something told him the feeling was mutual. Martha went on, "Anyway, I wanted to hang with you tonight."

Sam was touched. "Thanks." As they passed through the kitchen, he could smell her patchouli scent mingling with the last gasps of Mr. Foster's chili and a faint whiff of Jimmy's Pizza pepperoni. He breathed deeply. The un-dyed down of blonde hair on the back of her neck, some distance below him, caught the light from the stove. He felt a little tingle of gawky excitement. He grabbed cookies for them both to mask it. "What was my dad talking to you about?"

"He wants me to audition for the school play."

"Oh. Yeah. He's got that on the brain right now. Are you going to?"

Martha shrugged. "I dunno. What's it about?"

"Well, he told me," Sam confessed, "but I forget."

They went into the den. "So, how's the happy father?" Martha demanded. "I heard all about it. Let's see the kid."

Baby Bunny was propped in a corner of the couch. He passed it to Martha.

"It's heavy," Martha said. She accepted the doll with the same cautious distaste Sam's sister had shown lifting the uncooked turkey at Christmas.

"It's Baby Bunny," Sam said.

"Screw that. Something this ugly is definitely a Baby Teggy. Gawd, it's not exactly cuddly, is it?"

"Nope." The doll, inflexible, stared back at them. Sam explained his routine with the key, and how no one could help him.

"Gawd," said Martha again, brushing back some stray blue locks. "What a drag. So you'll have to bring it to Toronto tomorrow. Hey, my dad said he'd come." Martha's dad lived in Toronto; Sam had never met him.

"Oh. Cool," he said. Right now, he was more concerned with the show. "Anyway, I'm gonna have to look after Baby Bunny—"

"Baby *Teggy*."

"Yeah. And play at the same time. And everybody keeps saying to me, 'It's a warning. Just be glad it's not a real one.'"

Martha shuddered. "As if. I am so not ever having a baby. The real warning is, don't take Family Studies." She laughed. To Sam it was the sound of raindrops on crystal bells; at least, that was what he'd chosen for a secret song lyric he was writing. Martha turned the doll beneath well-bitten fingernails. "It even looks as old as Teggy. Look at all the cracks in it. Maybe it's his evil twin, turned into a cyborg at birth."

Sam laughed and leaned in to look closely, taking the opportunity to inhale more patchouli and pepperoni. Martha was right. In the lamplight, the doll's dull vinyl surface was seamed with black cracks and scuff marks, especially around the head and the key slot in the back. It looked as if a lot of keys had missed their mark. As babies went, this was an old one.

"Sam," his mom's voice carried down the hall, "we're going out for a walk. We'll be back soon."

They heard the front door close. Martha tossed the doll face down on a chair.

"Don't!" Sam swooped to the rescue, turning it upright. "It registers as abuse."

"Well, we wouldn't want that," said Martha. She turned to Sam.

"I like your hair," Sam said. Then they didn't say anything for some time. Baby Bunny began to cry. Sam managed to one-hand the key into its back without fully breaking the clinch. His drumming had helped with something, anyway.

Finally, faintly, they heard the front door open and the "we're home" signal of booted feet being stomped harder than necessary. Martha sat up and smoothed her T-shirt. Stretched across her chest were the words STOP STARING.

"Good move with the key," she said. "I bet my dad would call that multitasking."

Chapter Seven

"Left here," said Mrs. Foster grimly, over fresh electronic wailing, "and then it's supposed to be down one block."

Mr. Foster flicked the van's turn signal and led the small Hope Springs convoy south from what a sign told Sam was Queen Street, in Toronto. He got the key in and Baby Bunteg (or Tegbun; Sam just couldn't quite get his head around "Teggy") stopped, in the nick of time. The doll had been especially cranky on the way in, and in the confines of the van, its sudden outbursts were even harder to take.

"There it is!" Darryl pointed, his bare knees jiggling.

Mr. Foster pulled over. Sure enough, a neon sign announced CLU OCKIT. It hung over a doorway, beside what might have been a derelict dog-grooming salon. A group of under-dressed smokers huddled on the sidewalk in the freezing rain.

"Cool," said Larry. Excitement had made him more talkative than usual.

"I'm thinking scuzzy is the operative word," said Mrs. Foster. Clearly she didn't get it. Or maybe the doll was getting to her. She'd had to waken Sam four times in the night to tell him the stupid thing was crying. Two of the times had been after the two-minute abuse limit, and when Sam had reminded her and asked her to wake him faster, she'd been more than a little grumpy. Mind you, at his mom's age, she probably really needed her sleep.

Cars were parked. A sizeable contingent of kids and parents

gathered on the sidewalk; the boys had had to sell a minimum of twenty tickets to take part in the show. Sam pulled out the key. Baby Tegbun stayed quiet. The Hope Springers hustled back along the street with Darryl in the lead. As they passed the smokers, the distinctive aroma of another burning leaf mingled with tobacco.

"Ahhh, home cooking." The voice blared from the middle of the Hope Springs pack, more than loud enough for everyone's parents to hear. Sam winced. That would be Lotus.

He pushed quickly through the door to a stairway and was greeted by another unmistakable tang, one that said the puddles on the floor and stairs weren't the result of a leaky ceiling. This, thought Sam approvingly, was definitely rock and roll. Clutching his drumsticks, he started up—avoiding the wet.

Club Rockit was already crowded and booming. Celtic punk pounded through the sound system. At one end of the place, a low stage was lighted, complete with a sound system and a drum kit. Sam eyed it professionally as water plinked onto his head. Here, there definitely was a leaky ceiling.

"Oh, man," Darryl put down his guitar case, "can it get any better than this?"

Well, yes, thought Sam, dodging the leak. It could be way better if he wasn't carrying a computerized baby in a pouch. The show's promoter, sitting at a table at the back, seemed to agree.

"Is that baby gonna be all right like that?" He stopped counting tickets and squinted at Sam.

"Don't worry, it's not real."

"What, it's like a prop or something?"

"Kind of." It was easier than explaining, especially with all the noise; Sam was glad he'd brought earplugs. Baby Bunteg began his / her familiar wail. It was barely audible in the din of pennywhistles and crunch-distorted guitars; the promoter didn't even notice. Sam gritted his teeth, flicked the key into his hand, and inserted it in the slot without having to undo the carrier pouch.

This improvement was thanks to his mom. The sleepless night had kick-started her promise to think of something. Her first idea had been to get a substitute bracelet from the hospital, but no one she knew there was working on the weekend. Instead, she'd dug out Sam's old carrier from the cache that had included the highchair, and cut a large hole in the back for instant access.

"That will make it faster," she'd said. "But I don't think it will help you drum."

"Oh, it will," Sam had said, confident after his Friday practice. Drumming was one of the few things he was confident about. Others included being taller than most people and being able to sleep through almost anything.

The promoter told them they were on fourth out of ten acts. It was a good spot on the schedule. Perhaps pleased by this news, Baby Bunteg let him remove the key. As Sam turned away, he saw his sister Robin coming in.

"Sammy!" she cried, "and Computer Baby! Mom e-mailed me." She whipped out her cell phone and took a picture. "God," she said, "I am so glad I never took that course." She was with friends from university. Sam instantly felt less confident as he registered that two of the guys had major five o'clock shadow. They headed to the bar without commenting on his burden. It occurred to Sam that in the mishmash that was a Club Rockit crowd, a baby carrier might be just another new look.

"Is Martha here?" Robin asked. The first band was plugging in. "I want to meet her."

"Yeah. There's a whole bunch of people."

"Where's Mom and Dad?"

"I don't know. Over there somewhere, with Darryl's parents."

Robin glanced around the room, then, "Look," she said, as the band lurched into some kind of metal rap that made Rage Against the Machine sound subtle. Sam popped in his earplugs as Robin tugged her down vest and jersey away from the back of her neck. At the top of her right shoulder blade was a mark like a stretched horseshoe, with its ends curled out.

"Cool," he shouted back over the ranting. "What is it?"

"It's an ankh. It's Egyptian."

"Is it henna? How long will it last?"

Robin savored her own grin. "Forever, Sammy."

"It's a *tattoo?* For real?"

"Oh, yeah."

"Ho-lee. Why'd you do it?"

"Let's just say a statement needed to be made."

Sam gaped. Apart from the pre-Christmas debacle, the closest Sam had ever gotten to anarchic behavior was mismatched socks. "Do Mom and Dad know?"

"No, and no telling, either. I will, when the time is right. Hey, is that Martha? I know her from a party last summer."

Sure enough, Martha and Lotus were approaching. Sam put his ear to the doll. It was quiet.

Martha and Robin grinned at each other and did tiny waves back and forth. Lotus, who had shaved off one eyebrow and applied black lipstick for the evening, appeared monumentally bored. "God, they are so *lame*," she moaned to the world in general, as the first song shuddered to a halt. She pushed her rhinestone teardrop glasses back up her nose, which was pierced with a loop that hung to her upper lip. "You can't even dance to that."

Sam agreed, but he wasn't going to say so. "I've gotta have a cigarette," Lotus proclaimed. "C'mon, Marty."

Martha and Robin were giggling over something. Lotus tapped her on the arm and mimed smoking via two fingers pressed to her lips, while peering drolly over the rims of her glasses. Martha looked torn, then she followed Lotus to the stairs. "Back in a bit," she mouthed.

"What was *that*?" asked Robin, clearly unimpressed.

"That was Lotus."

"Lotus LeBlanc? I remember. I think she lost the likeability challenge."

Sam nodded in agreement as another tired metal riff shuddered out of the speakers.

Robin's own head-shaving, piercing, and combat-boot-wearing phase was ancient history now. One of the university guys returned with a beer for her. He had an ear stud and a barbed wire wrist tattoo to go with the five-o'clock shadow. "This is Grant," said Robin, in a too-cool voice. Too cool meant Grant was definitely hot. "My brother Sam, the drum god."

Grant nodded in a way that was friendly, but clearly also said, *I see you don't do five o'clock shadow.* Luckily, Amanda and Delft, part of the Hope Springs contingent, came by. "Good luck," Delft said. Sam watched Grant check them out. He was clearly impressed. Sam stood straighter. Then Grant saw that Sam saw. He looked back to Robin. Sam went to find his band.

Darryl and Larry were at the back, just inside the doorway of a dismantled washroom. Sinks, urinals, and lengths of chrome pipe were heaped in the middle of the floor like some kind of bizarre sculpture; the graffiti-covered walls gaped with holes. The punk sounds of band number two echoed crazily. The boys, oblivious, had their electronic tuners plugged into their instruments. Sam, feeling the first twinges of serious nervousness, snapped off a quick rhythm on the door with his drumsticks. Out front, he knew, the mosh pit would soon be in full swing, with Lotus and Martha and the other Hope Springs kids right in the middle.

Darryl unplugged his tuner and picked the un-amplified riff from "House Shaker," one of their original tunes. It was a tasty one. Now that they had moved into alternative sounds, they were light years beyond their first composition, written back in grade eight. They'd called it "Dragonsbreath"; Robin had called it "Farts of Fire."

"What if that thing starts crying?" Darryl packed away his tuner.

"Don't worry," Sam said. "I'm on it." For the first time, he wondered if he was.

They went out to watch band number three, the Emoshuns.

"Aww," Larry groaned, ten seconds in, "I hate emo."

"Who cares?" said Darryl. "They're setting us up perfectly. They're slow, we're high energy."

"That's true," Sam said. A drip of water landed on the back of his neck. He moved.

The Emoshuns, Sam realized, were not bad as emo went, but the slow tempos were making him more nervous. At least Baby Tegbun was quiet. On the other hand, he remembered, the longer the doll went without crying, the better the chance it would start while they were playing. He beat time to the tune against his thighs and thought pleasantly unpleasant thoughts about Mr. Tegwar. Meanwhile, he noticed the drummer on stage. He was keeping decent time, but he was twisting and rocking his head and torso around to what seemed to be a second, inner beat all his own. It was a style only slightly odder than Sam's own coping-with-computer-baby moves. If there was a God, Sam thought, maybe the world wouldn't have to see those.

With a final heartfelt strum, the Emoshuns nailed the coffin shut on their last ballad and trooped off. There was heartfelt applause from what had to be their contingent of the audience, plus all the parents who liked James Taylor. It was time for ADHD.

Sam, Larry, and Darryl huddled, and each put a fist into the center, knuckles touching.

"Ready?" said Darryl.

"Let's *play*," they chanted, and broke for the stage.

Chapter Eight

The first thing Sam felt on stage was the glare and heat from the lights. As Larry and Darryl plugged in, he settled onto the stool behind the drum kit.

That was when he felt the second thing: The seat was wet. He shifted uncomfortably and wondered just how hard the other drummers had been sweating. Or what else they might have been doing. At least the height was about right. He pulled the high hat a shade closer and tested the kick drum with a couple of quick thumps. Good. Snare, floor toms, the crash and ride were an easy reach. He snapped off a fill that took him around the kit to see how much give it had. The heads felt a little slack, but that was okay; easier than fighting against too much tension. His nervousness drained away, replaced by an eagerness to play. He squinted out from the stage and saw Martha and Lotus down front. Steve, Delft, Amanda, Alex, and the others were close by. All right, Sam thought. He resettled on the damp stool and rolled his shoulders against the baby carrier. The key waggled on the bracelet around his wrist.

Then he felt a third thing: Cold water was hitting his head. It trickled down the back of his neck. He looked up. A drop hit him square in the forehead. He flinched, and swiped at it with the back of his hand. Another drop hit his shoulder. It came to him why the emo drummer had been moving to two different beats, and why the seat was wet: The roof really was leaking and he was sitting under a slow-motion Niagara

Falls. Prudently, he moved his microphone. He didn't want to be the first electrocuted drummer in rock history.

He looked at the others. Larry and Darryl were looking back at him, ready to go. What could he do? He hunched against the impending deluge and nodded. Darryl strummed an A-chord. Sam tapped a three-beat intro. In a slightly quavering three-part harmony, they sang out, *a capella*:

"We're adhd
As you can see
Rock hyper-activity (it was hard to keep the beats right in this line)
Is our specialty
So dance and feel free
While we rock youuuuuuu ..."

Then, *two, three, four,* Sam beat rim shots on the snare, and *wham,* in unison they hit the downbeat of "House Shaker." By four bars in, Sam knew they were cooking. Despite the waterfall, he had nailed the tempo; everyone out front had instantly begun to dance. Larry, for once, was singing on key. Darryl's guitar lines were crackling. So, naturally, it was time for Baby Tegbun to cry. The music carried him past frustration. Just the way he'd practiced, Sam dropped one stick, scooped the key, and jammed it in, all the while playing high hat and kick drum with his feet and using his left hand to accent things up top. He knew Larry and Darryl could feel the difference. They both glanced back, then rocked on anyway. Sam grinned; it was working. More water plinked onto his head.

They brought the tune in to a solid round of whistles and applause. Darryl had been right; the emo band had set them up perfectly. As the clapping died away, Sam kept the key stuck in Baby Bunny's back and used his free hand to try and shift the drum stool away from the water. There was no room to move. *Please,* he thought, *please let this be a short cry.* In the relative quiet after the clapping he pulled on the key. The doll's bawling was suddenly front and center, its electronic oddness accentuated as it floated out over the sound system. Confused laughter came from out front. Damn, Sam thought, and pushed the key back in.

On mike, though, Darryl didn't miss a beat. He said, "I want to introduce the newest member of the band, on vocals. You just heard him now. Let's give it up for little Baby Tegbun!" He turned toward Sam, who got the cue and stood, pointing toward the doll with his free hand. There was more applause. "Baby Bunny isn't real," Darryl went on. "But he does like to sing. We just can't control when he does, so we'll play louder."

Playing louder was Darryl's solution for almost everything, but as Sam sat down, it seemed pretty good right now. Way to go, Darryl, he thought. A certain feeling told him more water had landed on the stool. Now it hit his head. He leaned back. Water plinked on the hand holding Baby Bunteg's key. He wiggled the key: a cry.

"Okay, this is called 'Radar Gun,'" Darryl said. Sam wiggled again. Perhaps pleased with Darryl's choice, Baby Bunteg stopped crying. Still leaning back, Sam yanked out the key and grabbed his other drumstick, just in time.

They rocked through the next three tunes as Sam kept on leaning. Out front, he caught glimpses of Lotus dancing into as many people as she could. Martha swirled by. Amanda, Steve, and Delft were popping in and out of the light. Faintly, at the edge of the light, he glimpsed his parents and Darryl's, grinning. Darryl was right; it couldn't get any better. Even the leak didn't bother him, as long as he angled back; reaching the crash-and-ride cymbals was a bit of a stretch, but hey, that was why he had long arms.

"Okay," Darryl panted as they finished "Starscraper," still winded by multiple attempts at the splits, "we're gonna finish ..." Sam leaned forward to adjust his snare and was instantly rewarded with water on the head. He leaned back again. Darryl said, "... gonna finish with our brand new song. This is called 'I Think I'm Me.'"

"Yay!" came a voice from the crowd. It had to be Martha's; she'd heard the song at a practice. Sam felt a little thrill of pride that she'd liked it, especially since he'd written the lyrics. It looked as if they were going to go out in style. With a big finish, they'd get invited back for sure. He counted time, then hit the lick that began the song.

Baby Tegbun began to cry.

Oh, no, Sam thought as he played, *Oh, God, no.* A mingled surge of panic and frustration hit him. There was no way he could play their big closer one-handed. It also lasted at least four minutes, depending on how much Darryl got the crowd involved. Which meant that even now he was less than two minutes away from failing his Family Studies assignment; thirty percent of the mark down the tubes, not to mention a total maturity mess-up. Could he get Darryl to cut it short? Darryl was deeply involved in playing his guitar under one leg while hopping on the other. Sam's foot slammed the drum pedal in frustration.

The place was rocking; they were rocking; *he* was rocking. ADHD couldn't blow it now. He couldn't blow it for them now. But how could he screw up majorly in Family Studies, the world's easiest course (except for Introduction to Pottery), in a semester that would count for university admission? And maybe blow his March Break-alone-driver's plan? And by abusing a baby? But it wasn't a baby, was it? His mind raced like a gerbil on an exercise wheel. He had to- What-if-Maybe-How-could-But-But-But—*AAAGGH*. He hit the tom so hard he felt the stick crack.

And then, under the music, almost right on the beat, Baby Bunny stopped crying. Sam was so surprised he missed the next beat himself. It was a miracle, but now was not the time to think about it. Ecstatically, he drove the song home.

There was a roar of applause. Whistles echoed.

"*THANK YOU,*" Darryl boomed over the mike.

Sam stood and instantly felt water on his head again. It didn't matter. Right now, nothing mattered. He wondered if he'd ever feel this good again. They piled off the stage. Larry and Darryl were grinning like maniacs. Sam could feel the huge smile pushing up his own cheeks. The next band was standing there, waiting to go on.

"Good set, man."

"Wear a raincoat," Sam laughed to the drummer.

They hustled back through a flurry of compliments. The promoter was standing by the bar. "Nice job," he said. "How old are you guys?"

"Sixteen," said Darryl, "but we can look older."

How, Sam wondered, but the promoter was already saying, "Sixteen? Very cool, then. You're theatrical," he said to Darryl. "I like that. People like a show." He looked at Sam. "It's a good trick, the one-handed drumming, but I'm thinking you could do more with the doll, y'know, like an Alice Cooper, Marilyn Manson thing. You could behead it or something, but I don't think it goes with your music."

Beheading was one of many things Sam had wished to do to Baby Bunny, but now all he wanted to do was return it to Mr. Tegwar, saved from failing. He said, "Actually, I have to give it back. It's for school."

"We can come up with something else, though," Darryl said.

"Great," said the promoter. "Anyway, we'll get you back. You wanna do the show in May?"

"Excellent," said Larry. He was almost getting verbose.

Darryl and Larry went to get their instrument cases. Sam pushed back into the crowd to accept congratulations, as a wail of feedback introduced the next group.

A certain amount of basking later, he was discreetly hand-in-hand with Martha.

"Hey," he remembered, "did your dad come?"

Martha fumbled for something in her bag. "Oh, no. Something came up."

Sam decided it was time to change into his spare, dry shirt. Lotus was busy butting heads on the dance floor, bringing the phrase "headbanger music" right into focus, so they edged off in search of Mrs. Foster, who had brought a spare T-shirt for him. They found her near the back of the club as the set ended. Sam pulled out his earplugs.

"Where are the washrooms in this place?" his mom asked.

Sam thought about where they'd tuned up. "Do you really want to know?"

"Oh," said Mrs. Foster. "What say we all go to a restaurant extremely soon?"

Sam looked at Martha. "That would be really nice," she said.

"I just want to change my shirt," Sam said. His mom dug into her bag.

"Presto. Well, Baby Bunny didn't give you too much trouble. That was very funny when Darryl introduced him. Or her. You looked like a proud father when you stood up."

"Oh, yeah? Well, I was lucky." He went on to describe the miraculous crying cure in their last song. And actually, it occurred to him as he slipped the carrier straps off his shoulders, the doll had been quiet ever since.

"Here, let me hold it," Martha offered.

Sam passed Snuggler and doll, and rolled his shoulders in relief. It had seemed heavier, somehow.

"Hey," Martha said. "This thing is soaked."

"Oh, my gosh," said Mrs. Foster, "is it ever! I thought it didn't wet itself."

"It doesn't." Sam touched the front of the carrier as Martha undid the snaps. It was sopping. "The ceiling was leaking up there, and I was leaning away from the drips."

Martha pulled out Baby Bunteg. Its cracked vinyl finish was slick with moisture. She gave the doll a shake.

"Don't!" Sam cried. "That's abuse."

Martha ignored him. She shook the doll again. In the between-bands lull, Sam heard a tiny, sloshing sound. Something unpleasant sloshed inside of him.

"Oh-oh." Mrs. Foster took the doll and turned it upside down. Water oozed from several hairline cracks and dribbled steadily from the exposed keyhole.

Baby Tegbun was soggy toast.

Part Two

Chapter Nine

"Do you know how much this piece of equipment cost?"

In the silence that followed, Sam watched Mr. Tegwar's Adam's apple bob above the precise knot of his necktie. Finally he said, "No, sir." Mr. Tegwar expected to be called "sir" if you did not use his name. It was number one on his list of classroom rules, printed on the board below the poster of the traffic sign that read ONE WAY, and in smaller letters beneath, *My Way*.

"They cost seven hundred dollars a-p-piece. The school can only afford them thanks to the generosity of the Yeswecan service club. And to have one of them ruined through gross negligence ..."

Baby Bunny lay silent between them on the raised front counter of the biology lab. The platform beneath the counter pretty much erased the height differential between teacher and student, so Sam had a close-up view of Mr. Tegwar's jutting jaw and bulging neck veins, not to mention ear and nose hairs.

"But it was an accident, sir. My mom wrote a note." Sam gestured forlornly to the paper that lay on Baby Bunny's lifeless breast and wished he could talk like Martha. Things were not going the way he'd hoped. Instead, he was living the nightmare of every student at Hope Springs High: Mr. Tegwar going ballistic.

"An accident." Mr. Tegwar pursed his lips; they disappeared completely. "This is exactly the kind of irresponsible behavior the exercise is designed to p-prevent. You were to treat that doll as if it were your own child."

"But sir—"

"Instead you have destroyed a sensitive and expensive piece of property. Clearly you understood nothing about this assignment. And you've ruined it for others. Not only do you get a zero, but I'll be speaking to the office about how you can best make this up to the school."

"But sir, I—"

"You'll have to suffer the consequences of your actions. Give me the key."

Sam held out his wrist.

He emerged from the lab as first bell rang. Morning music played over the P.A. It barely registered as he walked to his homeroom. He felt disconnected, as if, like one of those cartoon characters, he had just been sliced into little pieces, but so finely that not even he would see until someone jostled him and he crumbled into a pile of Sam-bits.

"What an asshole," Martha said. It was lunchtime and word of his doom had gotten around. For anyone who hadn't already heard, Darryl was once again busily recounting how "Sam drowned Baby Teggy in a rock club."

"So what will you have to do?" asked Delft.

"I don't know," Sam said, a little desperately. "I sure don't have seven hundred bucks." By now, he had begun to glue himself back together.

"And he didn't even read your mom's note?" Steve said, chewing vigorously.

"No." He watched Steve swallow. Sam himself was not hungry; in fact, at the moment, he couldn't imagine ever being hungry again. It also seemed to him vaguely disloyal that anyone else could eat right now. The injustice of it all launched him into a spirited rehashing of how unfair it all was. Was it his fault the stupid roof leaked? That he'd decided to take one for the team, for ADHD? For this, he deserved a zero on a major assignment in the semester that counted for early admission to university?

"Maybe," said Amanda, who was only slightly less practical than his mother, "you should have just given Baby Teggy to someone, anyway. You get three abuses, right? It only would have counted for one."

"No," Sam said, "I couldn't. I already had two abuses from when my mom didn't wake me up in time." He realized this was not helping his cause. He added quickly, "It's really tough in the middle of the night. You'll see."

"No, we won't," said Amanda. "Not without a Baby Teggy. I think you just saved the rest of the class, Sam."

"Oh, boy," Sam said. Delft smiled sympathetically. Or was she, too, just relieved? Still carrying his unopened lunch, he headed to the drama room to look for his dad. This was something he only did in times of dire necessity, usually related to a need for money. Mr. Foster was there, counting out booklets of some kind. He stopped counting and held one up as Sam came in.

"Scripts," he said, "for *The Amazings*. They finally came."

Sam registered this as the forgotten name of the school play.

"Well," his dad said, putting the counted scripts aside, "it sounds as if you've had yourself a morning."

Sam nodded.

"I was talking to Mr. Tegwar," Mr. Foster continued. "He read Mom's note, and he's calmed down, so it looks as if you won't be beheaded.

And, you'll be glad to know, he and I worked out a way for you to make this up that isn't going to cost either of us seven hundred dollars. He'll tell you about it." Mr. Foster paused to square the stacks of scripts, then put them on his desk. He tugged up the sleeves of his sweater. "Which leaves only two other points: First, it seems to me that while you tried, you could have handled this whole thing a little better. It shouldn't have been up to your mom—uh ... and me—to wake you in the night when that stupid thing cried. We've already been there, done that. And if you had been a little more with it then, you probably could have handed the damn thing off for a few minutes while you played, and not have had to worry about failing."

"I know, I know," Sam sighed.

"Good, because you might recall that we had a little discussion about maturity not too long ago and you promised to shape up. As *I* recall, Mom and I would like to go away for a couple of days at March Break and you'd like to start driving. This isn't the way to make it happen.

"Second: I bailed you out of this one, which I'm not going to do again. But since I did, you owe me big-time: You are now officially signed on as percussionist for *The Amazings*. Joining you in the pit band, which will actually sit up on stage, will be Mr. Tegwar, on clarinet."

Sam's mouth moved. No sound came out.

"Actually," said Mr. Foster, "I think your line to me is, 'Thanks, Dad,' and your line to Mr. Tegwar this afternoon is an ad lib, but here's a hint: Try including, 'I'm sorry.'"

"Thanks, Dad."

"Ni-i-ice."

Sam still wasn't sure what to expect when he got to Family

Studies that afternoon, but Mr. Tegwar was his usual grim self. On the lab counter sat a substitute for Baby Bunteg: a ten-pound bag of flour now rested in the carrier pouch, along with a whole new set of rules for its care. They sounded even worse than the originals; clearly the man's fiendishness knew no bounds. The air was thick with disappointment; a couple of kids even glared at Sam.

As the bell rang at the end of the period, Mr. Tegwar ordered Sam to remain behind. Sam approached the platform in deep slouch mode as Mr. Tegwar stood with his arms at his sides, almost as if he were standing at attention. His position blocked out most of a blackboard diagram of family groupings, leaving the word "nuclear" floating over his head.

Sam decided to go for his dad's advice. "I'm sorry about Baby—I mean, I'm sorry about the doll, I mean the Kinder 4000, Mr. Tegwar."

Mr. Tegwar stretched his jaw up and away from his collar and seemed to fix his eyes on a point somewhere just above Sam's head.

"Yes," he said, "well, this has been an unfortunate event." His voice clipped off the words. "I talked with your father earlier today and he and your mother's note indicate that you were somewhat torn between conflicting responsibilities." He flicked a look at Sam, then down at the floor, then back up again. "I, too, know what it is like to have a, uh, conflicted sense of"—he inhaled—"duty. Nonetheless, ch-choices mean consequences, however unintended. Consequences must be taken into consideration. Therefore, we have decided that you will be assigned twenty additional hours of community service, to be completed by the end of this semester."

Sam blinked. This was the deal? Twenty more hours ... and the school play. And homework. And getting ready for ADHD's May show.

And fetching and hauling for J. Earl ... "But I just finished my forty hours," he protested. "Sir."

Mr. Tegwar's hands clenched at his sides. "That was before you ki ... that was before you damaged school property. I am a member of the Yeswecans and I'll give you the telephone number of our president, Mr. Smithers. You may call him for work suggestions."

"That's okay, sir. I know Smitty." Glenn Smithers was a family friend who had married Sam's grade six teacher.

"*Mr. Smithers* will be hearing from me, also. I will expect a written report on your volunteer work by the end of semester."

Sam blinked again, despairingly. Wasn't the "volunteering" enough? He was already getting zero. Mr. Tegwar's grade ten biology class was dribbling into the room. The younger kids eyed Sam warily. You didn't want to get too close to someone getting Teginated. Mr. Tegwar was saying, "It will stand as a substitute for the original assignment. Now, I suggest you get to your next class."

"Yes, sir." Sam nodded and slumped out the door, unable to summon even his Survival Slouch. He was partway down the hall when Mr. Tegwar's last words struck him: substitute. Like a makeup assignment? Which meant he didn't have to bomb Family Studies?

He spun around, almost decapitating the school's shortest grade nine with his elbow, and hustled back to the biology lab.

"What do you mean, your homework is incomplete?" Mr. Tegwar was snapping at a tiny blonde girl with eyeliner overload.

"I didn't understand it," she said in a voice even tinier than she was.

"Then w-why didn't you come to me for help?"

Sam decided to say thank you later.

Chapter Ten

"Yeah, well, he's still an asshole," Martha said. "He shredded Hayley Dubrowski right in front of everybody this afternoon. I was in the can when she came in and she had eyeliner all over her face from where she'd been crying so hard. She looked like a raccoon." Perched on the Fosters' kitchen counter, she nibbled on a cookie. Today's T-shirt read TOO PRETTY TO LIKE MATH.

"Yeah, he's weird," Sam offered as a compromise. "But he did give me a makeup chance, and I bet Smitty"—he paused to punch Smitty's number into the phone—"gives me something easy to do."

Unfortunately, Smitty had nothing for Sam to do. After the fall food bank campaign, the Yeswecan service club kept a low profile until the Hope Springs a Leak crazy craft race down the river in spring. It was too early for that. Smitty said he'd tell Mr. Tegwar Sam had called.

"Yeah," Smitty chuckled, "he's a funny guy. Used to scare the daylights out of me in school. It took me a long time to get used to him at Yeswe meetings. I kept wanting to call him Mr. Tegwar."

"What do you call him?" Sam asked.

"Shithead," Martha put in from the counter.

"Scotty," said Smitty, on the other end of the line. "He's just this shy little guy, makes a bad joke once a year, works his butt off at bingos. Anyway, if anything comes up, I'll tell you."

Sam hung up, half relieved and half worried. He still had twenty hours to fill.

"You'll think of something." Martha hopped down from the counter and picked up her jacket. "Anyway, I'm going to the library. Lotus wants me to MSN her."

"Why don't you do it at home?"

"Mom cut me off 'cause I broke into Judy's room." Judy was Martha's sister.

"You broke in?"

"She keeps this padlock on her door."

"Why?"

"I don't know; she's paranoid. She says I take stuff."

"Do you?"

"Not that time. She was wearing the top I wanted. Anyway, whatever. I'm going to the library. I need something to read, too."

Martha, Sam knew, was a huge reader of anything that wasn't for school. Indeed, that was why she'd first spoken to him in early January, when she was still new to the school. He'd been slumped in the hall at lunch-time, reading *Slaughterhouse Five*, when a voice had said, "Oh, wow, somebody who reads. And it's not Harry Potter." She'd been carrying a copy of *Ghost World*. Books had led to music and the relative merits of anger thrash vs. original punk and New Wave. It hadn't hurt that Sam had had his drumsticks on the floor beside him. Music had given way to movies they'd heard songs in (a discussion that carried over two lengthy evening phone calls, as well), which had led to Sam's inviting Martha along on the group movie excursion that took place most Friday nights. This had led to shared popcorn and side-by-side seats, and, a week later, an accidental-on purpose finger linking in the back-seat dimness as everyone rode back from the mall, squeezed into Darryl's parents' van. Clearly it had been meant to be.

Now Sam was inspired. "I'll go with you. Mrs. Stephens is nice. Maybe she'll let me volunteer at the library."

"Do it," said Martha. "Then you could wipe out my overdue fines." He grabbed his coat. Processing images of Martha as a B&E artist and Mr. Tegwar as a shy little guy could wait for later.

Chapter Eleven

Mrs. Stephens was happy to let Sam volunteer. The library was not exactly on Sam's list of happening places, but it was warmer than dog walking (with no scooping, either) and it was a start. Plus, his mom complimented him on his mature response to a problem. *Oh, yesss*, Sam thought.

On Sam's first evening, Mrs. Stephens gave him a quick refresher course in the Dewey decimal system and helped him organize a roller truck of books for shelving.

"Okay," she said, "have fun. I've got a meeting, but Ms. Palmer can help with anything else." She glanced past Sam. "Oh, hi, Mrs. Kipling."

Sam heard an electronic hum. He turned to see a woman rolling by on an electric scooter. Mrs. Kipling made a rapid and complex series of motions with her hands, and responded to the hello with a string of obscenities that made high school sound like kindergarten. Sam stared after her. Mrs. Stephens seemed unfazed.

"She's a regular. She has some circulatory problems, so she needs the buggy. She also has Tourette's. You'll get used to it. She does her best to keep it down."

Sam nodded, still a little stunned. Mrs. Stephens smiled wryly. "We have a number of interesting patrons. My favorite right now is a man who's writing *War and Peace*."

"Huh? But I read that," Sam said. "It's by ... um ... Tolstoy."

"Uh-huh, and as soon as he finishes copying it out, it's going to be by him, too. Happy shelving."

Sam trundled his book truck off into the stacks. He emerged a while later to see a familiar figure at one of the computer terminals. Or at least an almost-familiar figure: Martha seemed to have dyed her hair black since the afternoon.

"Hi," he whispered.

"Hi. Just a sec." She tapped rapidly at the keyboard. A pile of young-adult novels teetered by her elbow. The top one was titled *Mosh Pit*.

"Are you on MSN? Mrs. Stephens told me it's against the rules."

Martha shrugged. "So rat me out."

"I like your hair."

"Thanks. What time are you done?"

"Not till eight."

"Cool." Martha stood up. Tonight her shirt read, YOUR WISH IS NOT MINE. "Hey, come over here for a sec. I want to show you something."

The door to one of the meeting rooms opened. Sam glimpsed Mrs. Stephens.

"I'd better go," he said. "Later, okay?"

He rolled his cart back toward the circulation desk. People emerged from the meeting room. This being Hope Springs, Sam knew them all. Apart from Mrs. Stephens, the first was Mrs. Doberman, who tried to run everything in town. Her last big project had been fixing up the Royal Theater. Before that, her project was piping Mozart through outdoor speakers on the main street, to keep teens from loitering. Now she was the one with the petition against *Nicely Naughty*. Next out was Mrs. Goldenrod, Sam's English teacher, and the third was Smitty, who winked at Sam. Before Sam could reflect on this odd combination, Mrs. Goldenrod was upon him.

"I didn't know you worked here, Sam. Don't you just love it?"

"Well, I just started. It's interesting," Sam said diplomatically.

"Oh, it must be—all these books. But listen, you're just the person I need to see."

Sam's Adult Scheme sensors flicked on. Instinctively, he moved to the other side of the book truck.

"We've just had a meeting. This spring we're holding a week-long celebration of J. Earl Goodenough and his work, right here in town. We're calling it Hope for J. Earl. Isn't that wonderful?"

"Yeah." Sam nodded warily. Everyone knew Mrs. Goldenrod was a J. Earl fanatic. This had caused Sam some trouble in the past. On the other hand, Mrs. Doberman and the great man couldn't stand each other. This, too, had caused Sam some trouble. Smitty, who never caused trouble, read only the sports pages and the TV listings. His Scheme sensors went to Full Alert.

"Now, we have some wonderful activities," Mrs. Goldenrod went on, "but what we really need is some youth participation, to show that J. Earl appeals to everybody. And since you know J. Earl so well, I can't think of a better person to ask to help out."

Sam hadn't heard such a horrible idea since Darryl's suggestion that ADHD perform in nothing but jockstraps. The fact was, J. Earl *didn't* appeal to everybody. "Wow," he said. "Gee ... I'm pretty busy just now. I've got this and a history ISU and school play, and I'm already doing stuff for J. Earl's work-in-progress ..."

Mrs. Goldenrod nodded, then added with fiendish nonchalance,

"It was just that I heard you needed some extra volunteer hours ..."

"Oh ... yeah. Right. Well," he improvised, "um ... could I think about it? I, uh, should ask my parents if it's okay and everything."

"Of course," Mrs. Goldenrod smiled. "Let me know." She headed off as an electronic hum and a gust of profanity announced the return of Mrs. Kipling. Sam silently repeated every word. The last time Mrs. Goldenrod had trapped him, he'd gone to a school-board meeting to say a J. Earl book shouldn't be banned. Instead, he'd ended up blurting that they shouldn't have to read the book because it stunk. And then no one had understood him, anyway.

There was a tap on his shoulder. It was Martha. "C'mon," she said. She led him deep into the 900s, down an aisle to the end. The big window there reflected them back against its blackness. Martha stopped, turned, and said, "Let's kiss."

"Here? But—"

"It's important to break rules. It should be a rule."

"I don't think—"

"Oh, okay ..." Martha sighed. She reached up and clasped her hands behind the back of his neck. She smirked at him affectionately. "You know one of the things I like about you? You're always trying to do the right thing."

Sam didn't know what to say. This sounded suspiciously like being called a wuss. It also didn't sound a lot like him, to him. And not just after pre-Christmas; Sam had always thought of himself as a bit of a rebel. Hadn't he been the first to wear mismatched socks as a statement?

"That's good for me," Martha went on, "'cause I go, like, Idiot Girl."

This was safer ground. "What do you mean?" he protested, holding her by the waist. "You're not dumb."

"Yes, I am. I'm a total screwup. Know why I came to the High after Christmas? I got suspended at St. Tiffany's so much I had to leave."

"Yeah, but what for?"

Martha shrugged. "Late. Weed. Not doing homework."

"Those don't mean you're dumb, just—"

"No, I am."

"What about those surprise tests, two weeks ago? You aced them."

"They don't count. They were in class, so you couldn't study. I tanked the rest."

"Why?"

"'Cause I didn't study."

"So why not study?"

"'Cause I'm a total screwup and I'm going to mess up my whole life, except you're good for me 'cause you try and do the right thing. Maybe it'll rub off."

He bent and kissed her.

As he felt her lips part, something flickered in the corner of his right eye. He risked a glance. Outside the window there was a stab of yellow light. It glowed on something personal you really wouldn't expect to see through a library window. Sam jumped. Startled, Martha turned, then shrieked. The light vanished as Mrs. Stephens and a couple of patrons hurried into the aisle.

Sam explained. Mrs. Stephens politely ignored how Sam and Martha were still hanging onto one another and called the police to report a flasher.

"Stick around libraries long enough, it pretty much all happens," she shrugged. "You have to take it in stride. Anyway, as one of my old bosses said: If they need a light, there can't be much worth seeing."

Chapter Twelve

Sam angled through the usual end-of-school chaos to Martha's locker. His backpack was heavy but his heart was light. It was the following Thursday, and life, thankfully, had settled down. The library had been tame. No one had been on his case about volunteering. Music rehearsals for *The Amazings* were still in the future. ADHD had written a new song, "Penguin Stew." He was carrying a pack full of homework, but it was under control. All of which meant that his maturity plan was back on track, so much so that tomorrow he and Darryl were taking the test for their learner's permits. Sam's parents had agreed to let him take the driver's ed. course over the March Break, although they still weren't committed to going away. This was progress, major progress. Sam and Darryl planned to celebrate it with everyone at the school's Valentine's dance Friday night.

Martha was stuffing the last of her books into her locker as Sam arrived. He admired her dump-and-slam technique; Martha's locker was even messier than his own and, being in grade ten, she'd had a year's less practice than him.

"Let's go," she said.

"Don't you have any homework?"

"I don't feel like it. I'm working at four-thirty, then hanging out with Lotus tonight."

"Doesn't she have any homework?"

"She's done. She texted me at lunch." Lotus went to school in

Cobourg and was apparently a major brain. "Anyway, who cares. What are you, my grandpa?"

"No, it's just—" Sam stopped. He'd been remembering Martha's saying he was good for her and he'd already glimpsed her in the school office that morning, doing makeup work for another assignment she'd ditched. Come to think of it, that had happened last week, too; right after their talk in the library, actually. But hey, she was right. He wasn't the homework police.

"—I've got a bunch," he finished lamely. "And I've got to study for my learner's permit. And I've got to give Darryl the 'do." Darryl, not content with freezing his legs this winter, apparently wanted to freeze his brain, too, with a Mohawk cut for his driver's license photo. Sam was the designated barber.

"He's really going to do it?" Martha laughed and made a face.

"He's really going to do it."

"What an idiot," she said, with a touch of admiration. "I don't call him the Zit for nothing, you know." Martha had an on-again-off-again regard for Darryl. In an off-again moment she had labeled him Zit On the Face of Life, or ZOTFL for MSN purposes. She took Sam's hand. "And we've got to go to J. Earl's."

"Ahh! Ri-i-ight. Geez, I almost forgot. Are you still coming?"

"Uh-huh. But we have to move. And we have to stop at my place first." Outside, they hurried through sunshine that lied about spring. "So I got the part in *The Amazings*," Martha said.

"My dad said you did really well."

Martha shrugged modestly. "Well, I used to take singing lessons."

"How come you stopped?"

"It's a long story."

They turned up Ravine Drive. Martha lived with her mother and older sister in a new section of Hope Springs. Sam found their house impressive; his family's place was old and always seemed to be in the midst of some renovation that his dad never quite finished. Martha's sister Judy was at the kitchen table when they arrived, bent over some homework. Judy was in grade twelve at St. Tiffany's.

"Hi, Sam."

"Hi, Judy."

The sisters ignored each other. Martha kicked off her runners and thumped upstairs.

Judy punched buttons on a calculator. "Do you take calculus, Sam?"

"I won't take it till next year," Sam answered.

"Oh, right. I keep thinking you're a year older, somehow."

"Probably because I'm tall," Sam said. "A lot of people think that." More thumping came from upstairs. Then some more. Judy called, "If you're looking for your weed, Martha, Mom found it."

Upstairs, Martha swore and slammed a door. Feet pounded back down the stairs. Judy calmly rose and plugged in the kettle.

"Do you want tea, Sam?"

"Thanks, but I've—we've—got to go."

Martha blew in. "Next time, I'll put it in *your* closet," she snapped, jamming her feet back into her shoes.

"Fat chance," Judy said without turning around. "That's what locks are for. That and thieves."

"Eat me." Martha pulled Sam out the door and slammed it behind her.

They started down the street. Sam was stunned. It felt as if he was walking alongside a small tornado. Did he and Robin ever sound like that? They used to fight sometimes and still argued, but this hadn't sounded like a sometimes. This had sounded like an all the time.

"What a drag," Sam offered. What was a drag? Well, all of it, but he thought he'd keep things vague to let Martha cool down. Martha said nothing. She was still in the middle of her own private storm. Sam looked for a neutral topic. As they crossed the bridge over the river, he asked, "Where'd you get the weed?"

Sam had no problem with weed. He'd had it a couple of times, with Darryl and Larry. Since they were rock musicians, it seemed almost mandatory. The result had been pleasing, but if getting there was half the fun, Sam figured they had lost out. Since none of them had ever inhaled anything before, the coughing, lost smoke, and raspy throats had been definite drawbacks. Plus, it was expensive. Darryl claimed to have been "really, really stoned," but then Darryl was wearing shorts all winter, wasn't he? Larry, as usual, had been more to the point when he said, "I think we wasted most of it."

Martha rolled her eyes at the question. "God. It wasn't even mine; I was just holding it for Lotus."

"How can she afford to buy? She doesn't even have a job."

"She scrounges her dad's roaches."

"Oh." Sam nodded as if this was an everyday thing. Maybe it was: He'd wondered more than once if his parents had toked back in the prehistoric days of their youth. It was barely possible, he supposed. After all, they'd had sex at least twice—unless he and Robin were secretly adopted.

"If she got a job like I told her," Martha snapped, "we could buy our own." Then, "God, my mom is such a bitch."

Sam had met Martha's mom numerous times; Mrs. Sellers had always seemed nice to him. Darryl had even called her a MILF, though this meant something a little different. He wasn't going to get into that now. Martha went on, "I wish I lived with my dad."

"Why don't you?"

"His place is too small 'cause he has to pay my mom so much money. But when this big deal he's working on comes through ..."

Sam had never met Mr. Sellers, only seen his picture: a slender man whose silver hair didn't match his young-looking face. In the picture, he'd looked very prep, wearing loud plaid shorts, a polo shirt, and a chunky wristwatch, standing next to some kind of zippy-looking convertible. Sam did remember he lived in Toronto. As he turned over the thought that she might want to move away, he felt her hand squeeze his.

"But I'd still want to get together."

The storm was over. Grateful, Sam squeezed back and turned to a more practical consideration.

"What will your mom do now?"

Martha waved the question away. "She'll yell at me; I'll yell at her."

This was not how things worked in Sam's family. "Won't you get grounded?"

"She can't *ground* me. I'd just go out anyway."

Sam knew he looked surprised. Martha laughed.

"Well, what's she going to do, lock me in?"

It was a good point, just one that he'd never thought of. It had always seemed to Sam that if you were grounded, you were. He said, "What if she locked you out?"

"No way; she'd be scared to. I'd just go to Lotus's, anyway. And then not call her. That would scare the shit out of her." She looked at Sam. "Boy, you haven't been grounded much, have you?"

"I have, too," he said defensively. This was not quite true, so he added, "I got grounded majorly right before we met."

"Yeah?" Martha's voice rose in interest. "What'd you do?" Oh-oh. There was no way he was telling Martha, of all people, what he'd done.

"Um ... well ... I can't say."

"Wha-a-at?"

"Well, it was a family thing, like. I promised my mom and dad I wouldn't tell." This wasn't true either. Actually, he'd asked his parents not to tell. But he was scrambling now. He guessed he wasn't making much sense, because Martha's face was squinched, her eyebrow piercing angled up in disbelief. He added, "It's why I'm being so careful now, too," then explained about driving and the March Break.

"Sweet," Martha said. "Wish I was going to be here. We're skiing in Quebec."

"If my mom and dad go, they're just going to Collingwood." Impetuously he added, "I wish we could go somewhere."

"Mmm. That would be nice." Martha slipped an arm around his waist.

He put his around her shoulder, glad she was happy again. "Robin got grounded, too," he said vaguely, just to say something now that he was in the clear.

"What, like, for the same thing? What were you doing?"

"No, no! Not then!" Even ignoring the odder angles of what he'd said, this was a sticky point for Sam because, in a moment of weakness, he'd tried to blame Robin for what he'd done. Luckily, Robin didn't know. Hastily he said, "I meant she got grounded a lot back in high school. She dressed really punk and had all these piercings."

"Cool," Martha said. "I like her." Martha's face lit up and she tugged his jacket. "Hey, know what we should do? Get tattoos, like Robin! It would be so cool. Robin's got one; Lotus has one; Steve's got one; Lucy ..." She ticked off the list on the tiny striped fingers of her gloves as they turned up Albert Street. J. Earl's house was near the top.

"But I don't think I want a tattoo." Sam was startled. Did he?

"Yes, you do! Think how much it would bug Teggy."

Bugging Mr. Tegwar was the last thing Sam wanted to think about. Okay, the second last: The last thing he wanted to think about was showing his parents a tattoo and watching his maturity plan flush down the toilet. On the other hand, thinking about *Robin* showing their parents a tattoo was quite fascinating. Which, come to think of it, might be what happened when she came home tomorrow for the university's reading week.

"Okay, forget Teggy. We get butt tattoos and flash them in *The Amazings*."

Sam stared. Martha burst out laughing. "Got you," she said. "I'm just joking. See? You're good for me. Everything's cool. I won't even get a tattoo." Then, "Oh, my God, what is *that*?"

Chapter Thirteen

They had arrived at J. Earl's. *That* was a white-topped convertible, very different from the one in the photo of Martha's dad. This one was roughly the size of Florida, and everything below the windows but the lights, whitewall tires, and license plates was wrapped in what looked to be aluminum foil and silver duct tape. Inside, Sam could see a fancy blue interior that looked futuristic in an old-fashioned way, from a time before seats had headrests and shoulder belts. Sam pointed this detail out to Martha, having become something of a car expert since starting the *Driver's Handbook*.

"Uh-huh." She was underwhelmed.

Sam's knock on the house door was answered by an immense black man in a gray T-shirt and warm-up pants. "Uh-huh," said the man. His bald head gleamed almost as much as J. Earl's did. "You the bookmobile?"

"Uh ... yeah!" Sam said, startled, but getting it.

"Excellent, my man. Come on in." Over his shoulder he called, "Yo, G-man, your book dude is here."

Sam and Martha stepped inside. J. Earl was in the living room, lying on a yoga mat. He was in sweat pants—and some discomfort, to judge from the language he used while sitting up. Sam guessed he was doing his hip exercises.

"Foster! It's about time. The books are in that bag in the hall, there."

Sam saw the bag. The other man passed it to him.

"All right," J. Earl panted, still sitting. He winced, then gestured with one hand. "Marvell Byrd, my physiotherapist, meet Sam Foster, my amanuensis, and—" J. Earl paused, looking from Martha to Sam.

"Martha," said Martha.

"Oh, sorry," said Sam, who'd been busy wondering what an amanuensis was.

"Martha," finished J. Earl. "I won't be getting up."

"That's okay," said Martha.

"My pleasure," said Marvell Byrd, shaking hands with them both. Sam could feel that his grip was deliberately gentle. The man was Sam's height and approximately five times as wide. Sam made a mental note to find his dumbbells.

"So, Foster, where's your offspring?" asked J. Earl.

Martha laughed. Marvell, moving back to J. Earl, looked at Sam, who now realized he meant the doll. "Oh," he said. "The project is done."

"I wish mine was," said J. Earl. Then, chuckling, he said to Marvell, "He was lugging around this doll programmed to cry."

"Uh-huh," said Marvell. He walked over and patted J. Earl's knee. "All right, bro, let's get that leg moving again."

Sam was turning to leave when Martha unexpectedly said, "You should tell how it died, Sam."

Sam shook his head urgently as J. Earl said from the floor, "How it *died*? C'mon Foster. I could use some distraction about now."

"Aw," Sam said, feeling a slouch coming on, "I just had an accident with it."

"He drowned it," said Martha.

Sam explained as quickly as he could.

"And now," Martha finished for him, "his teacher is making him do an extra twenty hours of community service. He has to work at the library and maybe on your celebration thingy."

J. Earl squeaked. Sam wasn't sure if this was due to Martha's pronouncement or the way Marvell Byrd was manipulating his leg. The great man looked up from the floor and fixed Sam with a piercing glare. "It's Elvira Goldenrod, isn't it?" Then, "Owwww! For the luvva God, Marvell, knock it off for a minute!" Marvell sighed and folded his massive arms across his even more massive chest.

"Mrs. Goldenrod wants me to help," Sam admitted.

"Damn! Why won't that woman leave me alone?"

Because she'd had a lifelong crush on J. Earl, Sam knew, having been told this by his parents. "But she has this whole committee, like," Sam said.

"Who else?"

"Well, uh, Smitty, Mrs. Stephens, Mrs. Doberman ..."

"Doberman? What the—" J. Earl was quite red in the face now, and his eyebrows were flapping, the way they did when he got worked up on TV.

Marvell said, "Hey, chill, G. You promised Dot you'd roll with this, man." Dot, Sam knew, was J. Earl's wife.

"But Doberman! It'll be a cat fight with Goldenrod. Plus, she hates me."

"Chill. C'mon, move that leg."

J. Earl ignored him. "Now listen, Foster. You have to help me. I need to know what's happening with that committee, and I'm not talking to them myself."

"But I'm not on the committee," Sam protested. "I said I'd think about it."

"All right, you've thought about it. Now join."

Martha cut in. "So you want Sam to volunteer for you, too?"

"What?"

"Well, if he goes to the meetings, you want him to report to you. You'd have to sign his volunteer sheet so he'd get credit for the hours."

"Sure, sure. Just keep me in the loop."

Martha smiled triumphantly.

Sam said doggedly, "I'll think about it. If I join, I'll tell you."

"Do that," said J. Earl. "No pressure, Foster, but I'm an invalid, Dot is busy, and I'm counting on you while I wrestle with my work-in-progress." J. Earl collapsed back on his yoga mat. Marvell shook his head and lifted the great man's leg again. Stretching and bending commenced.

"Just tell me one thing, Foster." This came from behind J. Earl's clenched teeth. "What the hell is Elvira Goldenrod doing handing out mechanical babies? I thought she was God's gift to English teaching."

"She didn't," Sam clarified. "It was another teacher, Mr. Tegwar."

"Tegwar?" said J. Earl. "Tegwar ... That ... I remember him. Scott Tegwar. Back when I came to town. All about Viet Nam, of course; that was the war, then."

"Mr. *Tegwar*?" Sam and Martha said it at the same time.

"Well, sure. He's an American, don't forget. Or he was. Anyway, he was up to his neck in it."

"Back in the day," murmured Marvell.

Sam was speechless. J. Earl resumed. "*He's* not on the committee, is he?"

"Mr. Tegwar? No."

"Good. Let's keep it that way," said J. Earl, as if he and Sam were running things. "There's enough nutbars now. And let me know everything. Got it? Everything."

Outside, Martha said, "Well, he's cool in a whacked kind of way."

"I guess," Sam said. Cool was not a word he would have connected with J. Earl. It was however, in a whacked kind of way, the word he'd use to describe the silver-wrapped convertible. It reminded him of something. He stared again as they walked by.

Martha was saying, "And was that wild about the Teginator, or what?"

"Uh-huh," he said absently. Then he knew. "Hey, have you ever read *Fear and Loathing—*"

"*—In Las Vegas*," Martha finished. "No, for, like, the fifth time."

This was one of Sam's all-time favorite books. The convertible reminded him of the car in the book.

"Hey," said Martha, "I'm over here. At the very least, you could thank me for getting you that sweet deal on your volunteer hours. Why didn't you take it?"

"Oh, sorry. Thanks. I'd just rather cover it with the library. I've done stuff for Goldenrod and Doberman before. Believe me, they're crazy." Then, "Hey," Sam flashed on an idea, "why don't *you* do it?"

"Oh, thanks. Does that mean I'm crazy, too?"

"No, but you could get some hours. How many have you got?"

"None. Screw that stuff; I've got, like, two more years. *I* don't have to be mature, do I? Anyway, I've gotta go or I'll late for work."

She rummaged in her bag and came up with her mp3 player and a pack of cigarettes. She caught Sam's dismayed reaction as she lit up.

"Since when do you smoke?"

"I used to last year, when I went to the other school."

"Well, what are you doing it for now?"

"Don't worry; I can quit whenever I want, just like last time. So don't give me a hard time—especially after I got you all those hours. Call me later, 'kay?" They kissed, then, with a wave of her multi-colored fingers, she was off down the street.

Chapter Fourteen

Sam put in his own ear buds and headed for Darryl's. Martha was a smoker and Mr. Tegwar was a Viet Nam vet. People kept changing. Why, he wondered, couldn't life be simpler? Like a learner's permit test (he hoped), or not getting a tattoo, or watching your sister explain to your parents why *she* got a tattoo.

He was still pondering these deep philosophical questions when he arrived at Darryl's. The Sweeney household was often busy, but right now only Darryl was home, and the place seemed oddly still. Not even any music was playing.

"You sure you want to do this?" Sam asked, kicking his sneakers onto the sizeable pile that always lurked by the Sweeneys' kitchen door.

"Oh, yeah," Darryl said unconvincingly. He kept his hands deep in the pockets of his surfer shorts. "It's going to look so cool."

"Well, where do you want to do it?"

"Here."

Sam left his jacket and J. Earl's books by the shoes. A chair with a bath towel draped over it sat in the middle of the kitchen floor. Over on the counter he saw a set of electric hair clippers and, beside it, a miniature, hand-held vacuum cleaner. The Sweeneys were prone to tools and gadgets; Darryl's grandpa owned the Handy Hardware outlet and both of Darryl's parents worked there. Currently Darryl was campaigning for his dad to install heating coils in the driveway to eliminate snow shoveling.

Sam picked up the clippers. They were quite light. He found the ON button and gave it a test press. The little machine jumped to life in his hand with a buzz like a hornet's nest. Darryl's head snapped around. Sam hit OFF. "Maybe we need some music for this," he suggested.

"Right," said Darryl, bravely. "Music. Definitely. Something punky, to go with my new 'do."

They settled for the Clash, turned up loud. Darryl sat himself in the chair and draped the towel over his shoulders. Sam stood behind him and looked down at Darryl's mop of reddish-blond hair. When Darryl had been younger he'd had an astonishing crop of freckles to go with his hair. Now they were gone; most of his hair was about to follow.

He turned the clippers back on. They blended in fairly well with "London Calling." "Ready?"

Darryl's head bobbed. "Just do it."

Sam began. Darryl's scalp was shockingly pale under his hair, and it was surprising just how much hair he had. And how far it spread, drifting and settling like a reddish-blond snowfall. Tufts of it stuck to Sam's hands, until they began to look as if they belonged to the Wolf Man.

It was also surprising just how hard it was to keep a Mohawk in a straight line. Sam wondered defensively if everybody's skull was as bumpy as Darryl's. Still, the wobbliest bits were in the back, where Darryl wouldn't see.

Sam went over the whole thing again, then turned off the clippers. The Clash boomed on.

"How does it look?" asked Darryl, over the music.

"Well ..." said Sam. The answer was, Darryl's head looked like a cross between a well-chewed cow pasture and the craters of the moon.

Also, Darryl had had long hair for so long that Sam had forgotten how big his friend's ears were. Now they stuck out like flying grapefruit. He preferred not to say this.

Darryl saved him the trouble. "Never mind," he said. "I'll just look in the mirror." He stood, cascading hair. "Be right back." Darryl tromped off down the hall, wafting a trail behind him.

Sam swallowed uncomfortably. He lifted a socked foot and shook it; a few of Darryl's hairs came loose; the rest stayed put. Experimentally, he blew on a Wolf Man hand. A small cloud of Darryl hovered briefly in the kitchen warmth, then drifted down to the tiled floor. The cd track ended. In the silence before the next song began, Sam sensed a greater silence from down the hall. He stepped gingerly over the hair surrounding him and wondered where the broom was. There was way more hair than the little vacuum could hold.

Then the music kicked back in and the outside door opened. Darryl's younger brother Ryan came in.

"Hey, Sam."

"Hey, Ryan."

"Watcha doing?" Ryan, who was in grade nine, had a reputation for common sense. This came mainly from never doing anything his brother did. Now his gaze slid to Sam's still-furry hands. Before Sam could answer, a voice behind him said, "Nothing."

Sam turned. Darryl stood in the doorway to the hall. The towel was in his hand and on his head was a blue toque, pulled down low; to just above his eyebrows, in fact.

Ryan's eyes widened as he took in the hair on the kitchen floor. "Oh, wow," he breathed. "Did you do it? Did Sam 'hawk you?"

"No," Darryl snapped. "It's just a trim, kind of. Never mind."

"Just a *trim*? C'mon, let's see."

"No. Never mind. Not right now."

"Aw, come on!"

"Maybe we should clean up," Sam put in, not at all sure he wanted a look under Darryl's toque. "Where's the broom?"

"In the closet by the fridge," said Ryan. "C'mon Darryl, let's see."

Sam stepped over a pile of hair and opened the closet. He could tell Darryl was going to give in and take off the hat (Darryl being Darryl, the attention would outweigh the embarrassment) which made now more than ever the time to keep busy. Even if he had just been following orders, he had a nagging feeling he owed Darryl something for his less-than-steady hand on the clippers. Leading the tidy-up might be just the thing.

He began sweeping. Behind him Ryan urged, "C'mon Darryl, don't be a wuss."

"No-oh."

"You'll have to show Mom and Dad."

"No, I won't. I'll say I've got a cold."

"Is it really bad?"

"No! It's like ..."

Sam swept harder. He knew what was coming next. Sure enough, after a brief stretch of uninterrupted Clash, Darryl said, "Okay, but just for a sec. And don't tell Mom and Dad."

Sam concentrated on hard-to-reach bits under the table. The broom clunked on chair legs. Then Ryan breathed, "Holy—"

"It's not *bad*," Darryl insisted. "It's just ... radical."

"I forgot your ears stick out like that."

"They don't stick out. It's just I have no hair."

"Where's the dust pan?" Sam put in, still looking down.

"Never mind," said Darryl, sounding anxious to move on. "We'll vacuum."

An instant later he was kneeling over the pile of hair with the mini-vac. Sam saw with relief that the toque was back on. He couldn't help but notice that the tight-fitting hat didn't make Darryl's ears look any smaller.

"That's not all going to fi—" Ryan was pointing out as the whine of the vacuum met the wail of the music. Darryl bent to his task with the fervor Sam had brought to his sweeping. Unfortunately, Ryan was right; the machine clogged almost instantly.

"Get a bag," Darryl ordered.

Sam pulled one from a container of plastic bags waiting for recycling and shook it out. It was too small. As he started to crumple it again, he noticed the lettering: *Nicely Naughty   A Tastefully Ti—*

"Hey," he said, involuntarily.

The brothers ignored him. Darryl wrestled with the detachable container.

"That's not the way you open it," Ryan said.

"It is, too."

"No, it's not."

Sam stuffed the bag away and got another. The brothers' wrangle continued. Which reminded Sam again that Robin would be home tomorrow. Meanwhile, Ryan and Darryl's disagreement had turned into a tugging match over the mini-vac.

"Let me!"

"You just—"

"No, don't pu—"

The machine squalled to life in their hands, almost in time to the music. The container tumbled free. A reddish-blonde cyclone engulfed them.

"Turn it off!" Darryl fumbled with the button. He and Ryan, clutching separate parts of the vacuum, stared wordlessly at the indoor weather.

From higher up, Sam watched with them. After a moment he said, "I think maybe I should get going."

Darryl nodded, extending his personal record for speechlessness. Sam simultaneously shrugged on his parka and jammed his furry socks into his sneakers. Still on his knees, Darryl asked a little forlornly, "Are you sure you don't want a cut, too?"

Sam shook his head. He didn't need to check his maturity plan for this one. He even had the right thing to say. "Nah. I don't want to steal your thunder."

Grabbing his backpack and J. Earl's bag of books, Sam stepped outside and quickly closed the door behind him. It was snowing. Not having a hat, it felt good to have hair.

Chapter Fifteen

"Stand on the line, please. Look at the camera. Don't smile."

Sam floated to the line. It was hard to keep from smiling. Could life get any better? It was Friday. He and Darryl had just passed their learner's permit tests. The school Valentine's Day dance was tonight, perfect for celebrating. Maturity was winning; he could already see himself helping his parents pack for skiing. *Soon*, he told himself, *soon*.

The lady in the license office tilted the camera slightly to accommodate Sam's height. There was a pause, then, "Thank you. Your photo card will be ready shortly. Next."

Darryl shuffled up. Sam stepped over to his dad, who grinned back at him.

"Stand on the line, please. Look at the camera. Don't smile. Hat off, please."

"But—"

"Sorry. No hats or sunglasses. Face and hair have to be fully visible."

Having a Mohawk for this photo had been the whole point of the haircut, but Sam could more than understand Darryl's reluctance. Darryl reached for the toque. Sam looked out the office window. There was a stifled squawk of laughter from the license lady. Mr. Foster looked at his toes to hide his grin.

"Thank you. Your ... uh ... heh-heh-heh-heh ... card will be ready shortly."

Darryl joined them, already re-toqued.

"I think you made her day, Darryl," Mr. Foster said. Darryl brightened.

"I guess that's one picture they won't forget."

"Which was the whole idea, no?" Mr. Foster reminded him. Sam had filled him in on Darryl's scheme.

"You know," Darryl said, "maybe I should keep it this way for *The Amazings*. You said we're going to be up on stage, right?"

Sam returned to earth. Ah, yes, *The Amazings*. He sighed. Mr. Foster had spent the drive to the licensing office talking about the show. Sam had always made a point of avoiding school stuff his dad was involved in. True, he and Darryl (and Delft and Amanda and Mr. Gernsbach) had been in the Maple Nitro band with him and some others back in grade nine, but that hadn't been for school.

Besides, Maple Nitro had played what turned out to be quite cool classic soul and R&B tunes; *The Amazings*, according to Martha, was a groaner: a creaky relic with only one hummable song. It was supposed to be a classic, too, but no one under five hundred years old had ever heard of it. Then there was the little fact that Sam was only doing this as payback to his dad for the Baby Tegbun disaster. Which raised the final, killer point: the Teginator himself on clarinet. It was bad enough being in the man's power for Family Studies every day. Why this, too? "Because you're percussionist in the school band, and because the score uses clarinet and Scotty isn't bad on the old licorice stick," Mr. Foster had said on the ride up. "It's perfectly logical. He wants to do it. Give him a chance."

"Why? He didn't give me one."

"Yes, he did. That's why you're doing community service hours and an alternate assignment instead of failing. Listen, Sam, he can be a fun guy. He's just too shy to show that side of himself much, and too old-fashioned to do it in class. This is a chance for you both to get to know each other better, and you should take it. He's a vanishing breed, you know; he's gonna be retiring soon. Be a little bit more mature about this; grab the experience. Later in life you'll be able to talk about the legendary Mr. Tegwar."

Sam had picked up on the maturity hint. He hated it when his parents did that.

Mr. Foster had signaled for a lane change. "I don't think Scotty'll know what to do with himself if he isn't teaching."

"The students have some suggestions," Sam had said darkly.

Now, however, even *The Amazings* couldn't cloud the horizon for long. The learner's permits were ready. The outside edges of Darryl's ears didn't quite fit in his picture. No one mentioned it. Instead, Mr. Foster jingled the car keys and pulled a quarter from his pocket. "Flip to see who gets first drive," he said.

What with avoiding left turns and speeds over twenty-five, it was a good deal later when Sam made a last, tentative turn into the Foster driveway. Snow crunched under tires. He realized he was actually partway onto the lawn. It didn't matter; Mr. Foster gave what could have been a sigh of relief. Sam felt exhausted but triumphant. They trooped into the house to find Robin already home for her reading week.

"Don't get your license yet," she said, starting upstairs. "I want the car tonight."

Sam followed her. "No problem. I'm going to the dance tonight, anyway."

"Oh yeah? At the school? With Martha?"

Sam nodded happily. "She's meeting me." Feeling perky again, he wondered maturely if he should grab his bi-weekly shave or go with what his dad called his "one o'clock shadow." Speaking of which, "Hey, are you still seeing that Grant guy? You know, with the ..."

"Maybe." Robin smiled and arched an eyebrow.

"When are you going to tell Mom and Dad about your tattoo?"

"Sshh!" Robin rounded on him. "Not so loud."

Sam took this to mean, "Not yet."

A groan came from down in the kitchen. Mr. Foster bustled back into the hall. "I've gotta go to the store. When Mom gets—"

"She already called. She's going to be late," Robin told him.

"Okay. And you guys can wait for dinner, right?"

"I'm going out as soon as you get back," Robin said.

"I've got the dance," Sam reminded him. "I'll just grab a sandwich." This was a bold move on his part, one he'd never been able to get away with before. His parents were fanatics about eating properly.

For once it paid off. "Okay," said Mr. Foster, opening the front door. "Then I don't have to race around like a madman. There's stuff in the fridge."

"Cool." His learner's permit; a snack for dinner: Sam felt awash in adulthood.

"Don't be long," Robin called after their dad. "I want the car!" She waited until they'd heard Mr. Foster tromp down the front steps, then said to Sam, "Look." She tugged up the sleeve of her jersey. A popular cartoon character was tattooed just above her wrist.

"Another one," Sam gasped. "Wow. How come?"

"Never mind." Robin rolled her sleeve down. "Just don't blab."

"No sweat." Sam washed his face, changed his т-shirt after applying extra deodorant, and had a slice of bread with peanut butter for supper. Then he headed for Darryl's. Walking, but like an adult.

Chapter Sixteen

School dances tended to be lame, but to Sam the point was they got everyone together, which made a good start for an evening. Larry, Amanda, Delft, Celeste, and Steve were already at Darryl's when Sam arrived, which meant the place had resumed its usual full-to-bursting atmosphere. Yesterday's hair avalanche had disappeared.

"Sam, look." Darryl whispered as the other kids spoke with his parents. Ducking behind the closet door, he whipped off the toque to reveal a microscopic buzz cut in place of the Mohawk.

"That looks better," Sam said diplomatically.

"Really?"

The answer was no, but Sam nodded.

Darryl quickly reapplied the toque to the fuzzy melon of his head and they all set off for the high school. It was a clear night, so cold the stars seemed to throb in the sky. Sam envied Darryl his toque, though not his shorts. They were almost to the park known as Monkey Mountain when an expensive-looking black car roared up beside them, pulsing with a thunderous hip-hop bass line. The passenger door opened, disgorging gangsta rap and a cloud of weed smoke, along with Martha and Lotus. Sam bent to see the driver. It was Lyle Doberman, son of the Mrs. he'd seen at the library.

Lyle was not well liked around town, though both Robin and Darryl's older sister had once thought of him as a hunk.

"How'd you get a ride from *him*?" Sam asked Martha.

"He's Lotus's cousin."

"I guess you got your weed back."

"No, silly. It was Lyle's. Lotus and I weren't even smoking. I only had one toke." She snuggled closer to Sam, which felt nice, although there was something hard under her jacket. "God, it's cold."

Lyle roared off. Sam was debating whether to tell Martha about his learner's permit or ask what was under her jacket, when Lotus barged up to him. Something buzzed angrily in her hand. "You're only cool if you shave off one eyebrow for Valentine's."

Sam stared. The buzzing something was an electric razor. It brought back memories of Darryl's head. "Maybe later," he said.

"Oh, don't be a wuss, Samantha." Lotus waved the razor at him, her nose ring gleaming beneath a streetlight. Sam knew she was shorter than he was, but she *was* a loomer.

"I'll do it." This came from Larry, breaking a brief conversational drought that had lasted since lunchtime.

They took the shortcut across Monkey Mountain. It was darker here, and the snow, rutted and hard packed from tobogganing, made for tough walking. Squeaks and crunches sounded beneath their slipping feet.

Martha reached inside her jacket and pulled something out.

"*What* is that?" Darryl came slip-sliding over. His shins glowed as white as the snow around them.

"Rum," said Martha, gripping the bottle by the neck. "Want some? Hey Lotus, where's the cokes?"

"Wait." Lotus polished off Larry's left eyebrow and shut down the razor. Then she dug out several cans of cola from the pockets of her parka. Martha opened one and poured out a healthy stream of pop that foamed and ate at the snow. "Hold this," she said to Sam.

Sam held the half-empty can while Martha glugged in rum. Some spilled onto his gloves. The dark smell of the liquor wafted up to him, along with a tingle of illicit excitement. Here, Sam thought, maturity would show. He couldn't wimp out and have nothing. At the same time, he couldn't get stupid; not with March Break hanging in the balance. Instead, he'd have just the right amount to show he could handle it. Fortunately, with booze Sam felt like an old pro. His parents offered him the occasional beer, or wine with dinner, and he'd sunk three brew at Amanda's New Year's party with no ill effects. "Where'd you get the rum?" he asked.

"Lyle." Martha's tongue was between her teeth as she poured. Lyle was a year older than Robin. Sam realized he must be home for reading week, too.

"There," said Martha. "Go for it."

The tin was substantially heavier. Sam took a sip. The taste was overpoweringly sweet, the tingle of the cola buried deep beneath the oily power of the rum. It felt like pure energy in the cold. He took another, bigger swallow and felt the sugar ease a hunger pang. He should have had more than that slice of bread, he reflected; some chips, maybe. Oh well, he could get something later. He passed the tin to Martha. She had some and passed it to Darryl. He drank and passed it on.

"Hey," someone said, "hear what Teggy did in Biology today?"

The Teginator's latest outrage was detailed as the can came back to Sam. There wasn't much left; he polished it off. It felt good to have something in his stomach. Another tin was prepped. Larry poured while Lotus held. Sam admired his own cleverness in pacing himself. Not that there was anything to worry about; a few ounces of rum and coke weren't like three beers. You just didn't want to get nabbed at the door for smelling of booze. He had a modest swallow as the tin came by. Pleased with his foresight, he rewarded himself with another swallow. This mix tasted even stronger.

Darryl had a swig, then coughed slightly. "Hey," he said. There was a tremor of enthusiasm in his voice that didn't go with a bald person wearing surfer shorts in February. Darryl was going to tell about his haircut; Sam could feel it. Years of experience had left him with a finely tuned sense of when a "Darryl" was about to begin, like those people who could feel it when rain was coming, or an earthquake.

Sure enough, still holding the can, Darryl began, "Guess what—"

At which point Lotus, who was either oblivious, or not in the mood for a Darryl, unceremoniously grabbed the can from his hand, drank, and announced, "Marty and I got tattoos this afternoon."

"Wha-a-a-at?"

"Where?"

"Let's see!"

"Yeah," Sam echoed, catching up. He'd been busy having a drink as another can came by. On second thought, it had seemed better to drink now. Then, for sure, you wouldn't smell later. "Let's see," he called.

"It's too cold," Martha said. "I'll show you later."

"OOO," everyone said. Sam grinned. That was his girlfriend talking.

"Yeah?" said Darryl, still trying. "Well, I got—"

This time Amanda cut him off. "Would it go with something from *Nicely Naughty?*"

Sam felt his grin get wider. He and Martha had a pretty strenuous necking life, although it tended to stay within certain limits. Still, it was flattering to be thought of as more daring. The can came around again. He had a celebratory drink. This one tasted like all rum. Easy, he warned himself, holding the drink in his mouth. It was good to know he was on top of things like this. If he stayed this smart, March Break was in the bag. He swallowed in anticipation.

"I bet Teginator goes to *Naughty* all the time," someone said.

This was one of the funniest things Sam had ever heard. It seemed like the funniest thing anybody had ever heard. Sam laughed so hard rum came out his nose. He had another swig to replace it. Amid the howls of laughter, he heard the *snick* of another pop being opened. Martha was grinning around a cigarette. "I'll pour," he said. His hand was like a rock. "Did you know guys think about sex every six minutes?"

"Guess what we heard about Teginator?" Martha blew smoke past this remark. "He's American and he was in Viet Nam."

"That explains it," said Amanda. "He's a combat psycho."

"Rambo Teginator!"

"No, seriously," said Celeste, "my uncle told me he heard he was like a commando guy and he married this girl from there and she died in the war and he's been twisted ever since."

"I heard that, too!"

"He wears camo underwear!"

"Camo thongs!"

"From *Nicely Naughty*!"

"Nah," Sam cut in coolly, "they don't sell them."

"How do you know?"

"I've been in."

"Get out. You have not."

"Have. A few weeks ago." Sam had a deep swallow as the can came to him. He thoughtfully wiped the rim on his sleeve before passing it on. "Mrs. Gernsbach invited me to," he added confidentially.

"Well then, I'm gonna go in," Darryl announced. "I know the Gernsbachs, too."

"That'll be the day," said Celeste.

"Know what they should do?" said Larry, looking a little lopsided with only one eyebrow. Sam wondered briefly why Larry had only one eyebrow. "Have a *Nicely Naughty* boat in the Leak race."

"Yesssssss!"

The Hope Springs a Leak crazy craft race blundered its bone-chilling way down the river every April. Sam had been in it some years ago, literally dragging along J. Earl, who had been reporting on the event and fallen into the river. Neither of them cared to repeat the experience. Now, though, all that was buried beneath a flood of shouted suggestions for a *Nicely Naughty* craft.

"... have barrels in, like, a giant bra!"

"Condom water balloons!"

"Guess what the mast would look like!"

"Eww, that is so gross!"

"And Teginator on board!"

This *was* the funniest thing Sam had ever heard. He lifted the tin for a last tiny swallow, just to show he wasn't sucking out. The tin was empty.

It didn't matter. They were moving across the park now, anyway, and the whole world seemed to Sam a wonderful place to be, though hard to walk in.

"Are you okay?" Martha asked.

"Uh. Huh. Fineyeah." He had a feeling that she'd said something before, something he'd missed while listening to the fascinating sounds of his own breathing. It occurred to him he also had a fascinating fact to share.

"Did you know that guys think about—"

"So you'll do it?"

"What? Sure." Do what, he wondered. Before he could clarify this, he was distracted.

"Hey," someone said, "anybody see that giant black guy around town lately?"

"That's Marvell," he said. "He's a physical, I mean, fideo, I mean video—"

The others' laughter was wrecking his concentration. "*Physio*therapist," he persevered. Let them try to say that walking up Monkey Mountain. Although, he realized, they now seemed to be on the sidewalk, just down from the high school. "You should see his car," he added. No one noticed.

"Here," Delft was passing something around. Breath mints. Sam crunched up three as they entered the warmth of the school. He bought his ticket, stomping down a runaway quarter on the first try. This was impressive, because the floor seemed to be on something of a slant. So was the gym; in fact, it seemed to be moving. It was the lights, he told himself. As they waded into the sonic assault echoing off the concrete walls, the whole place commenced a slow turn. He leaned a bit on Martha.

"Are you sure you're okay?"

He nodded. Maybe he'd drunk a *bit* too much. Fortunately, he was coping perfectly, just like in *Fear and Loathing*. Turmarity was the thing. Or was it matutinal? They dropped their coats on a bench. It felt hot already. Martha began to dance. Sam swayed a little. He thought about moving his feet, but it seemed like a better idea to leave them both on the floor. A strobe light began to flicker, splintering the room. This, combined with the bass line vibrating off the concrete walls, did something odd to his stomach. He closed his eyes. The room began to spin. He opened his eyes; the room splintered wickedly again. He needed to sit down. He turned, bumping several dancers, and reached for something to hold onto. What came to hand was Darryl's head. Sam slid to the floor, taking the toque with him. Darryl's scalp rose like a ghostly moon in the flickering lights.

On the way down, Sam grasped two other things, though in a different way. One was that a grim face was approaching jaggedly through the flashes: Mr. Tegwar's. The other was that he was about to be sick.

Chapter Seventeen

Sam opened one eye. Daylight stabbed at him. He shut it again quickly and groaned. This, too, was a mistake. The faint vibration in his chest brought back memories of the shuddering heaves that had wracked him into the early morning hours. Which brought back other memories, jumbled and mercifully indistinct. The rising moon of Darryl's head. The chill of a bathroom floor and wondering why there were no urinals. Someone's shoes; in fact, a lot of shoes, with a pair of black dress ones in the middle. And throwing up; a lot of that, too. Which brought him to the horrifying taste in his mouth—rum and coke laced with something that would dissolve tires.

He had to use the bathroom. Very slowly he levered himself to a sitting position on the edge of his bed. His brain did a barrel roll. Everything but his eyebrows hurt. He remembered Lotus and her razor. As he waited for everything to settle, he touched his forehead to make sure everything was still there. Then he rose, avoiding the bucket handily positioned beside his bed, and shuffled down the hall.

When he got back, his dad was waiting for him with a tray. On it was a large glass of water, a mug of clear tea, and a piece of dry toast. "Some night," said Mr. Foster.

Sam managed a nod. "Sorry," he croaked.

"Well, you should be," his dad said. "Parents aren't supposed to be pleased, you know, even if it does happen to most people sooner or later. Let's call it a learning experience. Can you manage some of this?"

Sam sat back down on his bed. He looked at the tray and shuddered.

"Try the water," said Mr. Foster. "It'll get the taste out of your mouth, help with the headache. You're dehydrated."

Sam had a tentative sip.

"Anyway," said his dad, "I'm not one of the people you need to apologize to. Maybe you can tell me who they are."

Sam applied what was left of his brain to this question. It didn't help. He looked at his dad, who raised an eyebrow. He looked at the floor, avoiding the bucket. "Um, I can't remember," he confessed.

"Let me help," said Mr. Foster. "You can start with Mr. Jensen, the custodian who had to clean up after you in the gym, and the hall. And the girls' washroom. And—"

"The girls' washroom?"

"The girls' washroom."

Well, at least that explained the no-urinals memory.

"And Mr. Tegwar," his dad went on.

Sam gasped. For an instant Mr. Tegwar's disembodied head was again knifing toward him through the strobe lights, as he ... as he—

"Did I ..." Sam asked, dreading the answer.

His dad nodded. "You did. We can get the pants cleaned, but I think you're going to owe him a new pair of shoes." Sam moaned. His dad continued, "And then there's Mrs. Moody; she was on duty, too." Mrs. Moody was the principal.

Sam looked up, stricken. "Did I—"

"Not on her. Just in her office as she was phoning us here at home. I forgot that one. You'll be seeing her first thing Monday morning, and you'll probably get a three-day suspension. Right now, bad as you feel, you need to get up. You're two hours late for work at the Bulging Bin and there are more books for J. Earl. Let's go; grab a shower. You buy the ticket, you take the ride. Welcome to responsibility."

Dutifully, Sam stood up. His head throbbed. At the doorway, his father turned.

"Just a little reminder, Sam, and I've given it to you before: A shot of booze has the same kick as a whole beer. I can't pretend I never screwed up as a kid and I don't expect perfection, but I expect a lot more smarts from someone who wants to stay alone for a bit on March Break."

Expect ... Wants to ... Did this mean there was still hope, or had he screwed up totally? It hurt too much to think about it.

Not many versions of hell featured cleaning out five-gallon peanut butter buckets while fighting a hangover, but by two that afternoon, it was Sam's personal one. It seemed to Sam that his mom almost smiled when she gave him the job. Robin, who'd been working cash, hadn't helped. Breezing into the back room she'd said, "Boy, were you ever a wreck. First time, huh?"

Elbow deep in a sudsy peanut butter bucket, Sam hadn't answered. It was too much trouble. It even hurt to listen.

"Don't worry; you'll grow out of it." Robin had leaned in close, then wafted something under his nose. "How about a little cottage cheese?"

Sam had gagged while Robin laughed and pulled the container away. "Don't worry, Sammy. I used to do dumb stuff, too."

When he was sure he wasn't going to vomit, Sam had croaked, "So when are you showing Mom and Dad your tattoos?"

Robin had smiled. Then she'd pushed two empty biscuit tins from a top shelf. The crash as they hit the cement floor nearly split Sam's brain in two. "Keep scrubbing," she said. "It suits you."

The fresh air helped on the way to J. Earl's. The great man didn't; clearly he was not feeling too well himself. It took him a moment to tune in, then he barked, "You're not getting the flu, are you? It's the last thing I need. I've got an important work-in-progress here."

When Sam admitted to a hangover instead, J. Earl perked right up. "Ohhh. Acting up, eh? Hair of the dog is what you need. How old are you, Foster? I should make you a Bloody Mary."

Sam swallowed hard. Mrs. Goodenough came to his rescue by offering him a coffee instead. Sam pleaded pressing homework and escaped with a "Thanks anyway."

He didn't come out of the house again until Monday morning. Despite calls from Martha and Darryl, and the fact that no one had outright said he was grounded, he'd opted for wallowing in homework, regret, and a letter of apology for Mrs. Moody.

After all, how could he have misjudged so totally? And now, of all times, with March Break coming up? And with a math test on Monday and his history ISU Tuesday. And how did you spell "incomprehensible"? Then another thought had struck him.

"What happens if there's a test or stuff while you're suspended?" he asked Robin.

"You fail it. There's no makeups for suspensions."

Sam's stomach had lurched all over again. He needed those marks, and not just for short-term maturity.

Stepping into the principal's office on Monday morning, clutching a letter of apology, he felt no maturity of any kind. He did, however, think he detected a faint odor of vomit in the air. Oh, God. He tried not to look for stains on the carpet.

Mrs. Moody got to the point. "Sam, you know you've earned a three-day suspension."

"I know. I'm really sorry, Mrs. Moody. It'll never happen again."

"It shouldn't have happened at all. I thought you were more mature than that."

That word again. "I thought I was, too."

"Do you want to talk about who else was involved?"

"I'd rather not say."

"How did you get the liquor?"

"Someone got it for u—me."

"Do you know that's a crime?"

"I do now."

"Good. Don't forget it. This is a tough time for a suspension, isn't it, Sam? This is an important semester for university admissions. I know you've got a test, an ISU presentation, and the beginning of rehearsals for the musical." Mrs. Moody shifted in her chair. "I also know you've never done anything like this before, and that you've volunteered to help Mrs. Goldenrod on her committee for the Goodenough celebration. So, instead of a suspension, I'm assigning you twenty extra hours of community service. I expect to hear how you're going to fill them. Now, if I were you, I'd get to homeroom, because your math test is first period."

A wave of relief broke over him. He stood up. "Oh, wow. Thanks, Mrs. Moody."

"Thank me by doing better. And Mr. Tegwar. I got the idea from him."

"I'll thank Mr. Jensen, too," Sam added.

"And Mr. Jensen. And Sam, if *anything* like this happens again, you'll be gone for a week, no matter what."

He raced from the office, eager for a math test for the only time in his life. On the way, he met three people. Darryl was the first, his toque firmly in place again.

"You didn't rat anybody out, did you?"

The second he met just as it struck him that he *hadn't* volunteered to be on the J. Earl committee. Mrs. Goldenrod smiled broadly as she came out of the staff room. "There's a meeting at the library Thursday night," she said. "See you there."

The third person was Martha, just getting to school as the bell rang.

"What happened?"

Sam told her.

"Cool," Martha said. "Now you can use that J. Earl deal I set up for you."

"Oh, yeahhh."

"And we can go to *Nicely Naughty* right after school."

"*Nicely Naughty*? What for?"

"To get Mrs. Gernsbach to sponsor a boat for the Leak race. Remember? You said you'd go in it with me."

Part Three

BALANCE

Chapter Eighteen

Mrs. Gernsbach was arranging a display of what Sam guessed were vibrators when he and Martha entered *Nicely Naughty*. The store had taken on a kind of tropical-getaway decor. Hawaiian guitar music floated out of the sound system and an embarrassed-looking potted palm tree stood near the window, festooned with plastic leis and thong underwear.

"Sam! How are you? I heard you weren't feeling so well there on the weekend."

"Oh, I'm fine, thanks."

Actually, he felt like the palm tree. Slouching, he probably even looked like the palm tree. The entire town seemed to know about his Friday mishap. While this had given his street credibility a welcome boost at school—he was now known as Chugger—it was making dealing with adults a pain.

The reason for their visit was making him no happier. No matter what he'd said when he was drunk, Sam did not want to go in the Leak race. Being on a *Nicely Naughty* entry might build his wild-guy reputation, but that was hardly what he needed right now. Besides, he remembered how horrible the race was. No matter what kind of crazy craft you had, you finished soaked and freezing, your hands and feet numb, and your butt tenderized by bouncing over the rocks. Plus, people threw water balloons at you right before the end. J. Earl had said it was like his first marriage all over again.

Meanwhile, Mrs. Gernsbach was looking at them and Martha was nudging him in the ribs. "Oh, sorry. This is my friend Martha."

Martha took over. "Hi, Mrs. Gernsbach." She extended a hand. "Wow, cool store."

"Why, thank you. You two are a little young to be in here, mind, so I can't sell you anything." She waved a rubbery green something in her other hand in an uh-uh gesture.

"Oh, no, that's not why we're here." Martha shook her head, managing to look gorgeous, innocent, and cheerful all at once. Beneath a tiny ski jacket she was wearing artfully torn tights and a mini dress, her now orange hair peeking out from under a knitted hat. "Sam and I have to do some volunteer work and we were wondering if the store would like to sponsor a crazy craft in the Leak race."

"The Leak race?" To Sam's dismay, Mrs. Gernsbach put down the green something and crossed her arms thoughtfully. "Now that might be fun ..."

"We'd build it and everything," Martha continued brightly. "And get people to ride it. But we were hoping you could help with the cost and maybe contribute some things for us to decorate with, to make it fun, you know, and advertise the store."

"What do you think it would cost?"

Martha pulled a folded paper from her coat pocket and smoothed it on the display case top. "Well, I tried to work it out. There's the entry fee. Stuff to make a sign. We can probably get a lot of the stuff for the boat ..."

Mrs. Gernsbach put on her half-glasses and the two of them huddled. Sam tried to look inconspicuous beside a voluptuous mannequin wearing a complicated lace-up garment that underscored its ample plaster breasts. He couldn't help but stare. Plaster or not, they were an incredible rack. Then the door opened and a trio of ladies from the bank gusted in, talking and giggling a little too loudly. Sam instantly pretended a deep interest in scented candles. Except that one looked like ... he reddened.

"I'll just wait outside," he called.

Martha joined him a few moments later, carrying a bag like the one he'd seen at Darryl's. "Bingo," she grinned.

Sam stifled a sigh. His last hope had been that Mrs. G. would say no.

"She even gave us condoms to throw to people," Martha enthused, waving the bag. "Here. You keep them. Nothing's private at my place."

Sam reluctantly took the bag. He looked inside at a plain cardboard box.

"Just stash it in your closet or something," Martha ordered.

"Gee," Sam stuffed the package in his backpack. "How do you *do* that?"

"What, throw condoms? Well, in the packages, I guess, or do, like, water balloons."

"No, I mean, talk like that? I couldn't do it in a million years."

Martha shrugged. "I dunno. It's fun. You just fake it; act adult, I guess." She got out a cigarette.

Acting adult did not seem to describe the Leak race. In fact Sam always thought the Leak race was a chance for adults to behave like kids. He shivered as they trudged back to Martha's. A way to warm up occurred to him; he wondered if anyone else would be home. As Martha flicked her lighter, he also wondered if she had any mouthwash; kissing after she'd been smoking wasn't his favorite. He didn't say these things, though. Instead, he said something that had just occurred to him.

"We can't do all this by ourselves. We're going to have to get some help."

"Well, duh." Martha laughed. "It's all set: Lotus and Larry and dorkhead Darryl. I mean, it was Larry's *idea*, remember? Wow, you really did lose it Friday. Anyway, Lotus is organizing all the rest."

"Lotus?" Oh-oh. Martha, in her enthusiasm, didn't notice.

"Yeah, and you know what? When Loti said she was in, Larry said right away that he was, too. He really likes her, huh?"

"He does?" Sam remembered a cryptic reference to a girl some time ago, and Darryl's advice to take the direct approach and snap her bra strap. He imagined doing that to Lotus, and the dismemberment that would probably follow. His mom diplomatically referred to Lotus as "sturdy"; Darryl called her a bull dyke.

"Gawd," said Martha, "can it get more obvious? He follows her like a puppy."

"Ahh," Sam said, as if he'd noticed this too, "right. I forgot." Now that she mentioned it, though, Larry never was around for ADHD practice.

"Hasn't he said anything?"

"Larry?"

"Oh. Right. Anyway, know what Lotus told me? He tried to snap her bra strap."

"Really?"

"Yeah. Stupid? Duh. But know what? I think she loved it."

When they got to Martha's, Judy was again in the kitchen. This time she was sitting at the table, books open before her as she typed something on a laptop. Martha shucked her coat onto the kitchen floor and swore. Judy ignored her. Martha made a face and turned the stereo on, loud. Then she rummaged in her backpack and lit up another cigarette.

"I thought you weren't supposed to—" Sam began.

"Know what? I don't give a shit."

The phone rang. Martha grabbed it. Even with the music, Sam could hear Lotus's voice boring out of the skimpy handset. *"Well, finally. I called, but I figured Miss Priss wouldn't give you the message."*

Martha took the phone and her cigarette and opened the back door. Cold air blew in. Music pounded. Judy clicked computer keys, stood, and began to close her books. Martha came back in.

"Why didn't you tell me Lotus called?"

"God, you just got here. And why would I tell you anything, anyway? See you, Sam." Judy walked out of the kitchen.

"Bitch," said Martha.

"Stoner," said Judy.

"I should probably get going," Sam said.

The Foster household was quiet, in contrast. It had been such an eventful day, and he was so intent on getting to his room with the condoms that it took him a moment to realize the place was, in fact, too quiet. Looking up the stairs, he saw that Robin's door was closed. His mom was in the kitchen chopping beans, with unusual zeal for someone who didn't like to cook.

"Your sister," she said without looking up, "forgot to keep her sleeves rolled down today."

Oh-oh. Sam was so startled he said, "Oh, wow. Did you see her back, too?"

His mom froze in mid-chop. She looked slowly at Sam. Then she put the knife down and headed for the stairs.

"Guess what," Sam called after her, attempting to lighten the mood. "I didn't get suspended!"

Chapter Nineteen

Robin was not happy about Sam's revelation, even though he pointed out that their parents would have found out sooner or later. "It's like having to go to the dentist or something," he said. "You might as well get it all done at once." This was, in fact, the opposite of his own belief that bad stuff should be avoided for as long as possible, but it seemed like a mature, adult-type thing to say.

"So, I should just pound you out now," Robin responded, "instead of getting you back in a million tiny ways for the rest of your life." Then she went and made a long and private phone call.

Sam could understand. He was burdened with maturity troubles, too. When would it all be over? When would ADHD practice again?

Thursday brought the first practice for *The Amazings*. It was an odd experience. Mr. Carnoostie, the school's music teacher, had the musicians in to listen to the score. Sam found himself sitting beside Mr. Tegwar. This kept him sitting up straighter. Since Sam had also just spent the last class with him, this was a lot of Mr. Tegwar to take. In fact, even Mr. Tegwar looked as if he might have had enough of Mr. Tegwar for one day. Though he was sitting bolt upright with his clarinet case primly in his lap, the lines in his face sagged with fatigue. His grim expression had lapsed into something approaching mournful.

"Now, the main thing to remember," Mr. Carnoostie said, "is the whole play is a parody. So we've got to have fun with the music. Keep it bright, brash, bouncy. There are not a lot of strong melodies, so we'll really have to help out the singers."

"Does parody mean there's going to be parrots?" Darryl went for the cheap laugh.

"Spare me, Darryl. Now, the other thing to keep in mind is that it was written back in 1958—"

"And I saw it in New York in 1964. I was in high school." This from Mr. Gernsbach, bustling in from his last school bus run. "Sorry I'm late." He turned to Mr. Tegwar, the only person he didn't know, and extended his free hand. The case for his bass guitar was in the other. "Hey man, Carl Gernsbach."

"Scott Tegwar." Mr. Tegwar rose to return the handshake. "I ... uh ... too, saw the show. In 1960, I believe, on my twelfth birthday."

"Get outta town," Mr. Gernsbach's gray ponytail bobbed as he nodded his head. "Can't say I liked it much."

To Sam's amazement, The Teginator smiled broadly. The lines on his face slipped away momentarily, taking a big chunk of years with them. "That was my impression, also. Of course, it was a long time ago."

Was it ever, Sam thought, mentally trying to do the math on Mr. Tegwar's age. No wonder the guy looked tired.

"Anyway," Mr. Gernsbach went on, "it musta had a helluva run."

"Well, it did," said Mr. Carnoostie. "Something like thirty years off-Broadway. After all, it's about young love versus tyrannical parents. Ring any bells?"

"Whoah, yeah," from Darryl. Sam mentally rolled his eyes. Darryl's parents were about as tyrannical as the Easter bunny. As the CD played, The Teginator sat quietly, listening and nodding. Darryl sprawled. Mr. Gernsbach settled into a Buddha-like nod over his T-shirted belly.

Mr. Carnoostie leaned intently into the music, elbows on knees. Sam tried not to shift around too much. Despite all the normal-person behavior, despite Mr. Tegwar's quiet acceptance of his apology for throwing up on him—he'd even refused the offer of new shoes—he still made Sam nervous. In fact, his normal-person behavior made Sam even more nervous, because it was so confusing. In some ways, it was easier when the guy was just plain unlikeable. Of course, this confusion was another reason not to like him. Which made it even more confusing: How could you dislike someone for not being unlikeable?

Anyway, what was *not* confusing was the music. It sucked. Apart from "Flickering Candles," the one hit song, there was nothing even hummable.

"We need a vacation," Darryl sighed as they slogged home afterward. "How long till spring break?"

Sam calculated. "Three more weeks."

"Do you know if your folks are going away yet?"

"Nope. I'm doing my best."

"How sweet would that be? They were really bummed about you getting drunk, huh?"

"Yeah," Sam sighed, "there was that and some other stuff."

"Well, Baby Teggy wasn't *completely* your fault."

"No kidding." Sam was a little annoyed that Darryl would think any of that was his fault. After all, he'd taken the hit for the band. "Anyway, that wasn't what I meant."

"Oh, yeah? What else did you do?" Instantly, Darryl was all ears—big ones.

"Aw, never mind." Sam groaned inwardly. Why hadn't he kept his mouth shut?

"No, what did you do? Did you break something?"

"Skip it."

"Come on, Sam. I'd tell you."

That was exactly the problem: Darryl would tell, everyone. Everything, with details, even if he had to make them up. The whole school would know in the time it took to type an MSN.

"No."

"You didn't have everyone over and wreck everything and not invite me?"

"Would I do that? No, it was on my own."

They walked on. After a bit, Darryl said, "Well, was it good?"

Sam didn't answer.

Suppertime brought a glimmer of hope. "What's Martha doing for March Break?" Mrs. Foster asked, as a bowl of pasta made its way around the table.

"She's going skiing in Quebec with her mom and sister," Sam remembered.

"And you've got driver's ed."

"Robin, on the other hand, will be up to her eyeballs in essays," said Mr. Foster jovially, taking a large helping of pasta. He was a man who enjoyed his own cooking.

"Thanks so much." Robin made a face back. She was wearing, Sam noticed, a short-sleeved T-shirt. Her tattoo grinned up at the world. "Can I have the car tonight?" Robin asked.

"As long as you drop Sam at the library for his J. Earl meeting. Speaking of March Break," Mr. Foster went on, "we have to let Mike

Carnoostie know if we're going to use his family's place for skiing, because his brother is interested, too."

Sam almost swallowed his fork. Was this it? He looked quickly at his mom. She was spearing some salad.

"When does he need to know by?"

"Well, ASAP," said Mr. Foster.

"Hmm." Mrs. Foster looked thoughtful.

"I thought Sammy had driving," Robin said.

"He does. He'd stay here."

"On his own?" Robin gasped theatrically. "Him? Well, it's your house." Clearly she hadn't quite forgiven him for the tattoo blunder.

"Let's talk about it later," suggested Mrs. Foster.

"Not much later," said Mr. Foster. "Mike needs to know."

Sam saw his mom shoot a look at his dad. He knew it would be safer to wait, but he had a feeling that it was all hanging in the balance right now, even if it was only six days after he'd vomited rum all over the principal's office. Before he could change his mind, he blurted, "I know I've done some really dumb stuff but I'm trying to make up for it, and if you let me stay on my own for two nights, it would be a chance for me to prove how mature I can be." He managed it in one long breath.

His mom raised an eyebrow. "You can prove how mature you are every day."

Help came from an unexpected source. "No, he can't," said Robin. "He's got teachers and volunteer people and you guys telling him what to do all the time. You can't be mature until you get on your own."

"I can't say I'm crazy about what *you* did on your own." Mr. Foster nodded at Robin's arm.

"Hey, it was my choice. Anyway, he's not going to get a tattoo while you're off skiing for a day and a half."

"No," Sam said virtuously. "I'll have driving. And Darryl would be here, too."

"I take it all back," said Robin. Then, "Just kidding."

Their parents looked at each other. Then Mr. Foster said, "Okay."

Mrs. Foster said, "There are going to be rules."

Chapter Twenty

"Wow—thanks, Rob," Sam said as soon as they were outside.

"No sweat," said Robin. "Except you owe me big time for the rest of your life." She handed him the keys and took out her cell phone. "Here, you drive. I need to check messages."

Sam was floating so high off the ground he didn't think he needed the car to get to the library. Still, he wasn't going to pass up a chance to drive. Oh man, he thought as he fastened his seat belt, he was officially Mature. He'd never try to blame anything on Robin again.

He got them to the library without a hitch, except for one jam-on-the-brakes instant at the traffic light downtown, when a black car swept past them. Robin looked up from her texting and shook her head. "Doberman. He always was a dork." She punched more numbers into her cell phone and commenced what was clearly a cozy private conversation. It was still going on when they pulled up at the library. Sam parked and got out. Robin waved goodbye as she walked around the car to the driver's seat, still talking. Sam fought down the impulse to give her a hug and walked into the library.

He was feeling so good he strode straight into the meeting room without a slouch defense. A number of people were already seated around a table, including Mrs. Doberman and Mrs. Goldenrod. Smitty was sitting with his back to the picture window, framed in the blur of shrubbery just outside. Beyond that, a ribbon of frozen river sparkled beneath a streetlight. Sam made a beeline for the chair beside him. Not

Acting Up |

111

only was Smitty a safe adult, the seat put him at a maximum distance from Mrs. Doberman, who was not. He might be feeling happy, but he wasn't stupid. As soon as he sat down, he noticed that everyone else looked more business-like, with pens and calendar notebooks. He leaned to Smitty and asked to borrow a piece of paper. Smitty obligingly tore a blank sheet from the back of his book. Sam extracted a slightly chewed pen from his pants pocket and joined the club.

Then, reminded by the river outside, he leaned to Smitty again. "I've got an entry for the Leak race," he whispered.

Smitty began to laugh when he heard what it was. Sam had been half-hoping that Smitty, as head Yeswecan, would say no, the whole thing was too out there. Now he felt unexpectedly pleased. If Smitty thought it was funny, maybe it was. It would be after March Break, and who cared about Lotus, anyway? He liked everyone else.

Down the table, Mrs. Doberman executed a no-nonsense throat clearing and said, "Let's begin, shall we? First, welcome. As you know, May eighth through eleventh has been designated Hope for J. Earl week here in town and we want to organize a fitting tribute to one of our best-known—"

"And loved. And most illustrious," put in Mrs. Goldenrod.

Mrs. Doberman acknowledged this with the world's smallest smile "—citizens."

"Yep, he's quite a fella," chuckled an oldster across the table.

"A great, great, man," Mrs. Goldenrod nodded. "A major writer, and a crusader."

"I think we're all agreed on that, Elvira," Mrs. Doberman said crisply.

"Plus, we want to do it before he croaks," said Smitty.

"Uh, yes. So, for our newcomers, I'm going to ask Betty Stephens to run down the events so far. Then we need to set up subcommittees to run them."

Mrs. Stephens smiled and lifted a piece of paper. "Here's what we've got so far." She ran down the list. It was all for old people. An evening at a local pub, devoted to J. Earl's war books. A screening of *The Moose Who Wasn't*, and *Sounding Off*, an NFB short about the great man, made back in the 1960s. A retired CBC-type Sam had never heard of (but all the oldsters murmured about) and the editor of the Hope Springs *Eternal* doing something about J. Earl's journalism. Finally, a big night for J. Earl at the Royal Theater, featuring a number of other famous Canadians Sam had never heard of, culminating in the presentation of a portrait to the great man himself.

A discussion began about who would organize what. Sam kept his mouth shut. This might be boring, but it could also be painless. If everything was for the ancient (how could he help organize a pub night?), he might not have to do anything but show up for meetings, look Mature and collect volunteer hours. He yawned and stopped listening. A few moments later, in the middle of a particularly intricate doodle, he sensed a change in the atmosphere. The air felt suddenly thick with good intentions. He froze.

"Well, those are all super ideas," Mrs. Goldenrod was saying, "but why don't we ask an expert? Sam, what do you think?"

Sam caught a mini eye roll by Mrs. Doberman. For a moment he was tempted to darn well show her. Then he remembered he'd missed all the suggestions. "Uh, could you just run over them again for me?"

Mrs. Doberman sighed. Mrs. Stephens re-explained that J. Earl had said he wouldn't visit the school or meet groups of kids, because of his health. This was just as well. Sam had been there the last time J. Earl had gone to Hope Springs High. A parent had been trying to have one of his books banned, and Sam and a camera crew had watched as J. Earl tried to nail a copy to the front door. Unable to drive a nail through the book, the great man had resorted to duct tape. Now the suggestions were: presentations by someone for young students at the library, readings in the high school cafeteria or on the morning announcements, an essay contest—the winner to read at the gala—an art contest, after-school discussion groups.

Sam chewed his lip as he listened. He could feel his pulse surge as the ideas got worse. If word ever got around that he'd helped with this, he'd be dog chow instead of Chugger. Doing art or—gag—essays would require actually knowing something about J. Earl or his work, and there would be teachers at the High who'd make it mandatory. And readings in the cafeteria? He shuddered to think of the roasting some poor clown would get, standing up there by the cash, reading *Snowshoe to Suspense* or *The Unflappable Owl*. Which led to a vision of who one of the clowns would be. He had to kill this now.

Still, he had to be careful; this was not a time to get Mrs. Goldenrod angry. Within him, a tiny voice urged, *Try and sound like Martha.* What would she say?

"Well ..." he said to say something, "I'm not sure *all* of those would work." Then he stroked his chin to look maturely thoughtful, a move of his dad's that he and Robin often parodied. The grownups waited. Geez, what more could they want?

"Ummm ..." he improvised. The attentive silence stretched on.

Desperately, he ran with the only thing that might spring anyone from school. "What if ..." he began, "uh ... you had high school kids, volunteers, like, come down to the library ... and read stuff to younger kids? That would show that they were into it. And maybe whoever helps could get volunteer hours? And the little kids could do the picture contest," he added, to pad things a bit. The little kids could handle that crap themselves; they probably wouldn't mind—after all, he'd just gotten them a field trip.

The grownups bought it, even though Mrs. Goldenrod insisted on daily readings on the high school announcements. Sam let it go; no one ever listened to the announcements, anyway. He was sitting back in his chair and registering that his shirt was soaked under the arms when gasps sounded across the table.

Mrs. Goldenrod and Mrs. Doberman were both staring, their mouths open. Mrs. Goldenrod had a lot of fillings. Mrs. Stephens was clamping down on a grin.

Sam cringed, thinking they'd noticed his armpits. Then he realized they were looking past him, out the picture window. He turned. Outside in the bushes, a familiar light glowed. The view was even clearer than the last time.

Chapter Twenty-one

Saturday afternoon at two-thirty, Sam hung up his apron at the Bulging Bin. He hadn't even had to work today and he'd done it anyway. He was on a roll; how mature could you get? With only one week until March Break, nothing was going to spoil his freedom. Or almost freedom—his mom hadn't been kidding about rules. Sam wasn't worried. He was feeling especially mature since reading a book about another Sam, called *The Maltese Falcon*. Sam Spade, the hard-boiled detective hero, could handle himself in a tight spot, too.

He said goodbye to his mom, resisting the urge to call her "Sweetheart," as Spade would have done (the man was a devil with women), then paused outside the store to turn up the collar of his coat, the way the actor Humphrey Bogart had worn his in the movie version of the story. They had it at the library. For a moment, he wished he had a fedora to tilt over his eyes.

He strolled to Jimmy's Pizza. Martha was about to get off work. He knew these streets like the back of his hand, the way Spade knew San Francisco. Granted, Hope Springs only had two blocks of downtown, but you worked with what you had.

Jimmy's, as everyone knew, was the worst pizza in town, but it was the cheapest, and Jimmy did a brisk trade selling slices to kids from lunchtime on. Besides, when it got hot and busy, there was the added bonus of watching Jimmy's Elvis-style hairpiece slide around. Today it was not busy. Martha was waiting for him, seated at a table, reading a book ambiguously titled *Junk*. Jimmy, who was a nice guy, pressed a slice with pepperoni and green pepper on Sam.

"Go ahead," he said, "eat. Look at you. God, you're a string bean."

"Thank you," said Sam, and, being hungry, he ate.

They walked back to Marvin's Family Restaurant. Martha slipped an arm through his and hurried him along.

"'Member what I said about Larry?" Martha said.

"Yeuh." Sam's mouth was full. "Wash the rush?"

Martha ignored this. "Well, it's official."

"Really? Larry and Lotus?" He swallowed. Larry could have been married with children for all he ever told anyone, but the girls' intelligence network thrived on this kind of thing. He passed on saying, "Poor Larry." Instead, he asked, "Is he still snapping her bra strap?"

They rounded the corner, still hurrying. To Sam's dismay, Lotus was in Marvin's, in the booth by the front window. She made her cigarette gesture, then rose.

"You go in," Martha said, fumbling out her own smokes, "We'll be one sec."

Lotus passed him on her way out. "Toodles," she said.

Toodles? What was that supposed to mean? Sam took off his jacket and sat in the booth. The restaurant was warm. Mrs. Marvin took his order for fries and a hot chocolate, over a background jumble of voices, crockery, and the Classic Rock Swap 'N' Shop on CHUC. Through the steamy window he watched Martha and Lotus, their cigarettes cocked with panache. It occurred to him that this was the kind of thing Spade would do, and instinctively he drew his upper lip back against his teeth, the way Bogart had in the movie. Of course, Spade would be smoking, too, and the world would be in black and white. He tried to see the scene before him in black and white. It was tricky.

Outside, the girls cracked up over some remark he couldn't hear. He forgot about Spade in the pleasure of watching Martha laugh. Then he wondered if they were laughing about him. Darryl was more likely. Then he saw Larry, crossing the street towards them. Larry always walked in a slow-mo glide that somehow emphasized the non-movement of his arms, as if he were a sleepwalker balancing something—a fruit salad, say—on his head. Now he cruised up, employing a last-second burst of armless speed to scoot ahead of a turning car. His hair bounced where it fell to his shoulders from beneath a checked tweed cap, but not even a finger twitched.

He stopped at the girls. Astonishingly, Lotus flashed what looked like a genuine smile. Then she hid it by drolly arching her remaining eyebrow. Equally astonishingly, Larry smiled and his lips moved for longer than a full second. Sam stared, vaguely aware that his own mouth had fallen open. It was true. Outside, the girls were gesturing toward the window. Larry came in.

Sam pulled himself together. "Hey," he said.

"Hey."

"Watcha doing?"

Larry shrugged. "Well, I'm here for the Leak thing. We're supposed to be talking about it, aren't we?"

They were? Sam had thought he was just meeting Martha. He was going to have to ask her about this. Mrs. Marvin arrived with his order and the girls returned.

"All right." Lotus shouldered her way in beside Larry and helped herself to some of Sam's fries. Her tongue stud and nose ring glinted unappealingly.

"What can I get you?" asked Mrs. Marvin.

Martha wanted coffee, Larry hot chocolate. Lotus, still chewing, asked for ice water.

"So," Lotus said loudly, "I've got it all planned. We're going to do it with inner tubes; big ones. Then we have to attach, like, a bed on top. Helium-filled condoms on the bedposts. And we've all gotta get wet suits. We're spray-painting them fl-l-lesh tones." She rolled the *l* lasciviously. "Marty and I will get kinky underwear from Gernsie the cow, and the guys will have paper leaves; you know, whaddyacallit, fig leaves. As if Darryl would even need one." She let her jaw go slack and looked at the ceiling to mime the stupidity of the idea.

Larry beamed. Sam, who had on occasion been critical of Darryl (though not for this reason) felt a flush of dismay. Off the top, he couldn't even decide what was more unappealing: prancing around in costume himself or contemplating Lotus in a flesh-toned wet suit and kinky underwear. His misgivings must have shown. Lotus immediately said, "What's the matter, Samantha, too hot to handle?"

Martha giggled and nudged Sam's foot under the table.

"No," he fumbled, "it's just that I thought—you know, I'd had some ideas myself. That's all."

"Like what?" Lotus took more fries.

Sam hid behind his hot chocolate.

"Never mind."

"Hmm. Stellar." Lotus did her jaw-drop-eye-roll-to-the-ceiling move again.

Sam swallowed the wrong way and began to cough. Martha pounded his back.

"I can get the building stuff," Larry offered, "and we can build it in my dad's shop. But I don't know about wet suits."

"Cool," said Lotus. "We'll start on Tuesday." Then, "Oh my Gawwwwd." She pointed a be-ringed index finger at the window.

Some beefy guys in snowmobile suits were stumping down the street. One was wearing a toque that stood straight up. It looked like the head of a rainbow trout. A fishy fabric eye gazed balefully back at Sam. The top of the hat split in a v, mimicking an open mouth; something that looked like an oversized fishing lure dangled where the pompom should have been. It was so ugly it was beautiful, like a horror movie so bad that it was funny. It was, in fact, the perfect hat for the Leak race. Wait till he told Smitty.

Lotus had a different take. "What this town needs," she pronounced, "is more gays. At least they have *style*."

Mrs. Marvin arrived with their order.

Chapter Twenty-two

"What was that all about?" Sam exclaimed when he and Martha were finally alone. They were walking to her house. "I thought I was just meeting you after work."

"Oh, Lotus needed a way to get Larry to get together with her. He's not exactly Mr. Talkative. So we figured, tell him we had to meet about the Leak race and then they'd go hang together after. And see? They did. Anyway, we had to plan before I go away for spring break."

"Well, you could have told me."

"Well, you could have got to Jimmy's on time. Then I'd have had a chance."

Sam let it pass. Then, as delicately as he could, he asked, "Are you ... uh ... sure you want to do this Leak thing? It seems like a lot of work."

"'Course I'm sure." Martha was indignant. "What's the matter? It'll be fun. And you promised, remember?"

"I know. It's just, well ... like ... I was ... when I ... oh, never mind. I just didn't like it very much last time." He told her about dragging J. Earl down the river. "And at the end, we crashed into Darryl's family's boat because Robin and Darryl's sister Melissa were racing to look good in front of Lyle Doberman."

"Lyle? Really?"

"Yeah," Sam laughed. "They thought he was a hunk. Can you believe it?"

Martha, busy with a cigarette, didn't answer.

"Then, after, we found out he was scoffing lawn ornaments all over town. You know, garden gnomes, fake deer, wind spinners. All that stuff. J. Earl had this fountain of a little kid that peed."

"What a riot! That is so cool."

"What, the fountain? Actually it was—"

"No, scoffing garden statues. What, did he put them downtown or something?"

"He was hiding them until ... well, it was complicated. Anyway, me and J. Earl and Robin and a bunch of us stole them back and stuck them on the Dobermans' lawn for garden tour day. His mom had a fit."

"What'd you do *that* for?"

"To get him in trouble! He was a total goof, taking everybody's stuff."

"Well, he was probably going to give them back. What'd you get him in trouble for?" She really sounded annoyed.

"Because—oh, skip it. You have to know him. Anyway, his mom can't stand J. Earl."

They walked in silence. Sam wondered what he had said to upset things.

Finally Martha said, "Want to get a movie tonight? We can watch it at my place."

"Cool. Hey, did you read *The Maltese Falcon* yet? I can get the movie."

Martha shrugged. "I tried. I want to read about real stuff, you know? Like us. Not old people."

"But the movie's pretty cool."

She smiled at him for the first time. "And let me guess: It's in black and white."

"Yeah," Sam admitted.

Her smile broadened sexily as she raised her cigarette. "Cool. I love black and white. The whole world should be that way."

Sam smiled back and relaxed for the first time in the conversation. It didn't occur to him until later that even black and white needed shades of gray.

Chapter Twenty-three

Lotus hadn't been kidding. Tuesday night found them gathered in the converted garage Larry's dad used for a workshop. Sam had assumed a relaxed approach would be taken to building a crazy craft, starting, say, the night before the race.

"So, what's this? Where the hell are the inner tubes?" Lotus grimaced behind her teardrop glasses.

Unfazed, Larry said, "I couldn't get inner tubes, but this will be even better. We'll be higher up from the water." He hefted a roll of the orange plastic mesh used as fencing at construction sites and shoved it eagerly at Lotus, like a giant bouquet of flowers. She took a step back as he said to her, "We'll use this stuff like super-strong netting and fill it up with empty plastic bottles for buoyancy. We make two nets, then tie this plywood over here on top—see, I've already drilled holes—for a platform, and then we can decorate it any way you want."

Everyone was impressed, even Lotus. It was also more than Larry had ever said in his life.

"We also have to drink a lot of pop," Sam put in, thinking of the bottles.

"This can be done!" Darryl proclaimed.

"We've got some empties to start with," said Larry. He opened a bin at the back of the workshop. It was filled with plastic drink bottles. Larry was one of a large family. "My dad takes them to the transfer station in the truck every month," he explained. Then he turned back to the mesh.

"My brother and I made one net already." He looked at Sam and Darryl. "You could start filling it over here." He looked shyly at the girls from behind his hair. "And maybe you can help me make the other one."

Sam and Darryl dragged the orange netting over to the bottle bin. As they worked, Darryl whispered to Sam, "You were right, he really does like her!"

"Yeah, but tell me why."

"Maybe her tongue stud helps his flossing."

Sam stifled a laugh. Across the garage, the girls were helping Larry cut more mesh on the cement floor. The heater was on and coats were off. Martha stood up, saying, "So, do you think we can make it so it looks like a big bed?" She was wearing a T-shirt that read: *This is where I nod and act like I'm listening.* He admired its contours carefully before noticing Lotus's proclaimed DON'T EVEN THINK ABOUT IT. Don't worry, thought Sam, I'm not.

Over the hollow clunking of the bottles, Darryl said, "So, what nights are your parents going to be away?"

"Monday and Tuesday. They gave me all these rules to demonstrate maturity."

"You'll notice they didn't say *our* maturity," Darryl said.

Sam flicked a glance at Darryl's toque. "Actually, they did."

"Oh."

Sam knew Darryl was on thin ice, too. Despite the teen code of silence, his parents had not been oblivious to his involvement in the dance episode. They were also less than thrilled about his haircut.

"Anyway, there's rules. We have to promise no one comes over; we get to driver training on time; and we have the place cleaned up by the time they get home."

"Sweet."

"Oh, and no drugs or drinking. And no Internet." Especially no Internet, but Sam didn't say that. Given his recent past, none of this seemed like much of a sacrifice. He wondered how long he'd be known as Chugger.

"This can be done!" Darryl said again. He stuffed more bottles into the meshing. The bin was nearly empty and there was a lot more to fill. Larry had made a big net, which was fine with Sam. He wanted something a lot sturdier than the last craft he'd been on. He tossed in the last bottle. "What now?" he called over.

"Squeeze 'em right down to the bottom," Larry instructed. "The more we get in, the better it floats."

Sam and Darryl tried to oblige. The stiff plastic scraped Sam's hands. Still, the end of the net swelled out considerably.

"Fantastic," Lotus cried. "We'll have them stick out the front like giant boobs. Oh, we gotta make nipples for them!"

Sam sighed, and tried to remember how he'd gotten into this. Then he remembered why he couldn't remember how he'd gotten into this. There was definitely going to be no drinking while his parents were away.

"It's like *Fear and Loathing in Las Vegas*," Darryl said enthusiastically. "I can feel it. The bad craziness is just beginning."

Chapter Twenty-four

Sam managed a mature coast into spring break, which unfortunately began with a last wheeze of winter. Wet snow fell on Saturday night. Martha left for skiing with her mother and sister. Larry and family went south. Late on Sunday morning, Mr. Sweeney took Darryl and Sam to the grocery to pick up some supplies for parentless living. The Fosters were due to leave Monday morning, as soon as Sam left for driver's ed. They got chips, microwave popcorn, hot dogs, buns, pizza pockets, peanut butter, bananas, milk, juice, and iced tea.

"Get the two-liter bottles," Darryl reminded him, thinking either about their crazy craft or just the importance of excess in PFL: Parent-Free Living. Unfortunately, iced tea did not come in two-liter bottles. Sam grabbed two cases instead. They were boxes, really, each containing twelve cans. As long as there were other beverages, it seemed to be enough to get them through two nights.

They loaded everything in the back of the Sweeneys' family van. It seemed to Sam a tamer, yet satisfying version of the trunk full of drugs at the beginning of *Fear and Loathing in Las Vegas*. A mature version. He climbed in the back seat, beside the supply of DVDs they'd already rented.

"Could you please drop me at Goodenoughs'?" he asked Mr. Sweeney. "I have to shovel their snow." It was his last chore before PFL.

"Sure," said Mr. Sweeney. "You hear that, chauffeur?"

"Yup." Darryl was making elaborate preparations in the driver's seat, including a final adjustment of his hide-all toque. Sam envied every move except the toque shift. Tomorrow, he reminded himself. Driving heaven was just around the corner.

The snow was heavy, and already melting. It felt like shoveling homework. Sam was sweating by the time he finished the job. He climbed the newly cleared steps to the front porch and knocked. After a long moment, the door was answered by an equally sweaty J. Earl, resplendent in his exercise clothes.

"Foster! C'mon in."

"Oh, that's okay. I just—"

"C'mon in!"

Sam obeyed. Inside, the house looked different. An exercise bike stood in the middle of the living room. A rime of books, papers, and CD cases, some topped with empty mugs or glasses, covered various surfaces and had begun to creep across the carpet. A towel hung from the back of a wing chair. The smell of burned food lingered like a bad memory.

"Dot's in Victoria, visiting her daughter," said J. Earl. "She needed a little break after putting up with me for the past couple of months." He headed for the towel. Sam could see he was moving much more freely than he had been even a week ago. "Feeling good, Foster; feeling good. I'd be a new man if it weren't for my damned work-in-progress."

"So why write it?" Sam asked, offering the Martha approach to homework.

"Because the publisher gave me a hell of an advance and I'm not paying it back. But I'll tell you, it's getting bloody tiring making up good stories about myself." J. Earl lifted the towel and wiped his face.

Sam felt his own brow wrinkling. He was sure he'd heard Mrs. Goldenrod say a memoir was writing about stuff that had actually happened to you. He had no time to puzzle over it, because J. Earl was pushing on, talking about reorganizing the work around pieces of music that had been important to him at different times in his life. Sam could relate to this, though he didn't think he'd ever confess that his favorite music when young had been one of his mom's old ABBA records. J. Earl, on the other hand, was a jazz buff. Jazz was a genre Sam found only slightly more compelling than Inuit throat music.

"... and then call the whole thing *It Don't Mean a Thing*," said J. Earl, "after the Ellington song. Whaddaya think?" He tossed the towel onto the couch.

"I guess." Sam tried to make this sound thoughtful. He remembered to stroke his chin. Sensing more was needed, he asked, "Are you writing anything about Hope Springs?" and then regretted it instantly. J. Earl might think he was asking if he was going to be in the book. This would sound sucky. Although, come to think of it, he wondered if he *was* going to be in the book.

None of this seemed to occur to the great man. "Nary a word," said J. Earl. He winked roguishly. "Too hot to handle, if you know what I mean. I cut a bit of a swath through the '70s." He picked up a glass of water and had a healthy swig. "I wasn't long divorced and the times being what they were, let's just say I had a few, uh, dalliances. Oh, yes," said J. Earl, not for the first time, "there was a time when Goodenough was good enough."

Sam smiled back uncertainly. He tried to imagine a younger, ladies' man J. Earl, with hair, and maybe some love beads, bell-bottom pants. It was a toughie.

"By God, it might be fun, though," J. Earl's eyebrows were flapping as he walked with his glass. "Stir things up in a few households around here ... heh heh heh. I could call it *Ain't Misbehavin'*. No, *In the Mood*." His eyebrows fell. "The problem, of course, is that the main household that would get stirred up is this one. This was all long before Dot and I got together, but, still. She knows some of these people."

Sam nodded as if he understood completely.

J. Earl stumped into the kitchen. Sam glimpsed pots on the stove and what seemed like a lot of dishes.

"How's that gal of yours?" J. Earl called over the sound of a tap running.

The telephone rang, saving Sam an answer. Clearly in a jaunty mood, the great man scooped up the receiver and intoned, "Underwater Aviation."

At the sound of the caller's voice, he grimaced. Then he stared at the ceiling and muttered something that sounded to Sam like, "Speak of the ..." After a moment, he cut in, "Uh-huh ... well, she's away for a few days ... *No*, I don't think that would be a good idea. I'm writing right this instant and I can't be disturbed. So, until Dot gets back, any communicating you need to do with me, you do it through Sam Foster. Goodbye."

J. Earl slammed down the phone. "That damn committee, trying to bury me before I'm dead. I dunno why Dot made me agree to it." Then he brightened. "Ha! But we showed them, didn't we?"

"But," said Sam, "what—"

"That's the spirit, Foster. I knew I could count on you. Just keep 'em away from me. Oh, and here's ten for the driveway. Geez, I gotta get Marvell over and help me clean up."

Chapter Twenty-five

Monday morning, Darryl called for Sam. They headed to the high school. Mrs. Foster's final instructions were still ringing in Sam's ears: "And the phone number you can reach us at is *right here* … We'll be home after supper Wednesday, to a *clean house* …" His dad was loading the van as she spoke; they'd be long gone by the time he and Darryl got back from driver's ed. He'd done it. Maturity had paid off. PFL was just around the corner, and a driver's license not far behind.

It even felt good to walk to school on a holiday. The morning was gray and almost mild. The streets seemed deserted; the puddles had skins of ice, but water splashed and gurgled in the storm drains. Their voices echoed as they made their way down the empty hall to an open classroom door. A handful of grade elevens, including Amanda, Delft, and Steve were sprawled at desks in varying states of grogginess. Standing at the front of the room, fiddling with a TV / video player on a rolling stand was an immense man with a shiny bald head. It was Marvell Byrd.

"Hey-y-y-y," he said, looking up. "The library dude. I thought it might be you when I saw the class list." His gaze shifted to Darryl. "My man, that is some serious hat."

Darryl grinned uneasily beneath his striped toque, perhaps afraid that he might have to take it off. But Marvell merely rubbed his own head with a massive hand and said, "I am a hat connoisseur myself."

"I thought you were a physiotherapist," Sam said, then thought,

Dumb, dumb, dumb.

"Oh, I am," said Marvell, "and a driving instructor. Short-order cook, personal trainer, dry-wall taper, bill collector, bouncer, catalogue model. Whatever pays the bills, bro. I have been many things since my glory days. Keeps life interesting. All right. Park it and let's get started."

Half the class was trooped out of the room with another instructor, to spend the morning actually driving. Envious glances followed them. The rest would spend the first part of the day in the classroom and drive in the afternoon.

The classroom part of driving lessons turned out to be quite boring, except for one video about a guy who advocated honking the car's horn at every conceivable opportunity. It was quite old and unintentionally funny.

"Geez," said Amanda. "If everyone did that, you'd have horns honking all over the place. Nobody'd pay attention. You couldn't tell who was honking at who."

"Sounds like high school," sighed Delft.

By noon, eyes were glazing over, and one of Darryl's legs was bouncing uncontrollably. Marvell collected a True / False quiz and announced lunch. "Thirty minutes, people; then the rubber meets the road."

Darryl and the others immediately headed for Little Hope Variety. Sam, too hungry to wait, opened the lunch his mom had made for him. Marvell Byrd, opening a bag of his own, said, "By the way, thanks for putting in some time with the G-man yesterday. It really picked him up, you know, what with Dot away and all."

"It did?" Sam was surprised. He'd thought that what had picked

J. Earl up was yelling at whoever had phoned.

"Oh, yeah," Marvell nodded fiercely. For an instant, he looked spectacularly intimidating. Sam remembered a couple of the jobs he'd listed. Marvell said, "Yeah, gotta get over there today myself. What kinda shape is the place in?"

"Well ... " Sam wasn't sure whether he should be accurate or diplomatic.

"That bad?" Marvell cackled. "Hey, I *know* the dude. G-man and I go back a long ways. This helping him out with his physio and shit is some payback time for me."

"Where do you know him from?" Sam asked.

"He wrote about me. I was his award-winning article: *Cracked Back: the NFL tackles a kid from Nova Scotia.* Got him this magazine award and a national radio gig."

"You played in the NFL?" Sam was impressed.

Marvell nodded curtly. "One season. Oakland, 1985."

"Why'd you stop playing?"

"They cut me in camp next year. Couldn't pass the medical. I'd been taught to hit, like, stick 'em, you know? Get the *hel*met in there." Marvell made a twisting jab with fist and forearm that made Sam feel as if his own body was a small, dry twig. Marvell suddenly splayed his fingers vertically and gestured at them with his other hand. "Well, I'd stuck 'em till I overstressed the vertebrae in my neck. Doctors told me, one wrong hit, I'd be crippled for life. So I was done."

"Oh, man," said Sam.

Marvell wolfed down half a sandwich. "But that's where G came in, see? I'd got me some coverage here in Canada for my ball scholarship and getting drafted and such, but he wanted to know about me now that I was *down*. First, I wasn't so thrilled 'bout that, you know? I mean, someone shows up like he's my pal, then wins a big award and a job telling the world I'm a loser and I'm still in Oakland breaking arms."

"Breaking arms? I thought you couldn't play."

"Never mind; long story. Let us say I was not in a *positive* place for a long time, you know? Did a whole lotta things I'm not too proud of. Point is, G, he surprised me. The man didn't quit. Kept on checking me out, slipping me a few bills, kept after me, you know, saying, 'C'mon and *do* something, Marvell. Get your game on, man; I gotta do another story.' He about wore me out until I finally started to get my shit together. I owe the man."

A babble of voices sounded somewhere down the hall. Marvell nodded at Sam's desk. "Hey, you eatin' those carrots or not?"

Chapter Twenty-six

After lunch, Marvell led Delft, Darryl, and Sam out to the parking lot. Marvell's massive tin-foil convertible sat in one of the spots; he stopped instead at a red compact. Sam felt a twinge of nerves. This was It, or close to It, a time for Maturity and a steady hand. He was happy to let Delft drive first.

Sam and Darryl piled into the back and Marvell took the front passenger seat, where, it turned out, there was a second set of pedal controls. Sam, already bent like a paper clip in the tiny rear space, involuntarily drew in his breath as Marvell climbed aboard. The car sagged. The man took up more space than an air bag in a safety video. His head, now covered by a crocheted skull cap, seemed ready to burst through the roof. "All right, Delft," said Marvell, "let's run it down."

Delft nodded. "Adjust the seat. Fasten my seat belt. Check the mirrors. Start up ..." She turned the key and the ignition caught. "Parking brake off. Foot brake on. Car in Drive. Signal. Check my blind spot. Pull out." She eased them smoothly out of the parking spot.

"It does not get any better," said Marvell.

Delft turned out to be more than a good singer; she was a good driver, too. Following Marvell's directions they puttered around town, the big man interspersing encouragement and instructions with chatter about his plans for the house he was building, summers in Nova Scotia. It was a bit like a soothing radio show, plus, it kept Darryl's mouth shut and his eyes on the road. Darryl, too, was a good driver. Sam began to wish he'd gone first after all, instead of having to follow two winning performances. Plus, his back was killing him. He wiggled and bit at a fingernail.

"Take it easy. You look like a praying mantis, all hunched like that," Delft laughed from beside him. "But a nice one," she added quickly.

Back in grade nine, Sam would have given anything to be squished into a back seat with Delft. He'd had a major crush on her when they'd both been in Maple Nitro. Then he would have found being compared to a stick-like insect romantic banter of the highest order. He would also have been a mere six foot one and thus more comfortable. Now, infinitely more experienced, he knew Delft was just kidding, to help him relax. She was nice that way. It worked, too.

He stopped nail-nibbling and smiled. "I may never walk again."

"You won't have to," Delft said. "We'll be driving. I mean, we all will be."

Finally, Marvell had Darryl pull over. Sam unfolded himself from the back seat. Delft helped push him out. He did a life-saving stretch as he and Darryl traded places, then looked into the car. The driver's seat was too far forward for him to even get in. "Is it okay if I adjust the seat from out here?" Someone his own height would understand the problem.

"You're the quarterback," said Marvell.

Sam found the lever. The seat slid back, whacking Darryl's bare knees.

"Hey!" Darryl protested.

"Live with it." Sam was already folding himself behind the wheel. "Okay," he said, hands already busy. "Seat's done. So, I fasten my seat belt, check the mirrors—"

| Acting Up

136

"This is uncomfortable," Darryl complained. Sam saw in the mirror he was grinning. He carried on: "Take off the parking brake, step on the other brake, shift to drive—"

The shifter wouldn't budge. Sam tugged at it. Nothing. He tugged again. Mystified, he looked at Marvell.

Marvell said, "It helps to start the vehicle first."

Chapter Twenty-seven

The phone rang as the first peanut butter sandwiches were made. At least, Sam was pretty sure it was ringing; with the stereo cranked on *Pinkerton* it was hard to tell. He peered over the first couple of iced tea empties. Sure enough, the little red light was flashing. He grabbed the cordless phone, stepped over Darryl's hoodie, and hustled upstairs, where it was quieter.

"Hello?"

It was Robin. "Mom wanted me to call and see how you're doing. I'm calling."

"I'm fine. Geez. We just got back from driving."

"Did you remember to start the car?"

"Ha ha." This was not the time. He ambled aimlessly down the hall.

Robin said, "Okay, I'm done. I've got too much work. Don't do anything I'd do."

"Like get a tattoo?"

"Ha ha." Now it was Robin's turn. "Anyway, that's only half why I'm calling. Tell Mom and Dad I'll be down to cover the J. Earl thingy at the theater."

Sam peered idly through the doorway of their parents' room as she said this. As usual, it was ridiculously tidy, except for a crumpled plastic bag by the wastebasket. Feeling virtuous, he stepped in to dispose of it.

"We won't be at the thingy," he reminded Robin. "*The Amazings*

138
Acting Up

starts the same night." This was the one blessing of doing music for the play. "Anyway," he said, picking up the bag, "that's not till May. Hey, you're not coming down for—Holy shit!"

"What?" from Robin.

"Um ... well I ... Geez! There was this bag on the floor in Mom and Dad's room and I turned it over and it's from *Nicely Naughty*!"

"Get out of town!" Robin crowed.

"That is so gross," Sam shuddered.

"What, that they have sex?"

"Well, like I knew that they'd *had* it—"

"Brilliant deduction, wonder child, or we wouldn't be talking."

"We could have been adopted."

"Hey, I was around when you were born. You ain't adopted. After I saw you, I hoped *I* was adopted."

"Ha ha. But I didn't think that they still—"

"Do it?"

"Yeah. They're old; it's kinda pervy. And know what, there was a bag like this at Darryl's house, too. In the recycling. I mean, can you imagine, everybody's parents—"

"Too much information," Robin cried. "I don't want to know. What really sounds pervy is you spying around for sex-store bags."

"I am not spying around. It was an accident."

"Yeah, right. What were you asking me?"

Sam had to think back. Oddly, his question connected, sort of, to the digression.

"You're not coming down for the Leak race, are you?"

"No, it's right in the middle of exams."

"Good."

"Why? Are you in it?"

"Never mind."

"I probably won't be able to see your play, either."

"Why not? You'll be home by—hey, how come you have to cover the J. Earl thing? Won't school be over by then?"

"That's the point, dumb one," he could hear Robin savoring the words. "I'm covering it because I got a summer internship at the *Star*. That's where J. Earl used to write a column. It's summer in the city for me, Sammy. Listen, just tell the folks I called. I'll phone when they get back. I e-mailed but they never check."

"I know." Once, before his pre-Christmas disaster, Sam had gotten in trouble for e-mailing his parents that he was staying over at Darryl's, instead of calling. Talk about unfair. Was it his fault they never checked their messages? "Okay. So, like, congratulations."

"Thanks. Oh—gotta run. Going out."

"I thought you had a ton of work."

"Well, we still have to celebrate, don't we?"

"We?"

"Grant and I."

Sam rubbed his cheek reflexively. "Is he an intern, too?"

"Among other things. Let me know if you find out what they bought at the store. Bye."

Sam punched the off button, stuffed the bag in the wastebasket, and clumped back downstairs, determined to do no such thing. In the kitchen, Darryl was making his second peanut butter sandwich, clad in boxers only slightly shorter and less garish than his surfers. In fact, the only way Sam could tell for sure that they weren't surfer shorts was because the shorts were on the counter.

"I hereby declare this a Pants-Optional Zone," Darryl called over the music. Sam flashed him a thumbs-up, dumped the phone, and kicked off his own cords. Serious listening and bad DVD watching was always more comfortable in boxers. This seemed to be a law of nature, in the same way that the film from a disposable camera would always include one shot of someone's butt. It was nice to be back in the land of normal.

"'King hell, man," Darryl said, "I think it's time for *Vegas*."

"Go for it," said Sam, making his own sandwich. "Don't forget the money."

Strewing Monopoly money around the room had somehow become part of the ritual of watching *Fear and Loathing in Las Vegas*.

Darryl shut off *Pinkerton* in mid-wheeze. Sam licked excess peanut butter from his fingers, then wiped them on his boxers. He grabbed his sandwich and headed for the den. In the momentary silence as Darryl put in the DVD, he heard the peanut butter knife clatter to the kitchen floor from its almost-balancing point on the edge of the counter. Sam plopped onto the couch. There'd be plenty of time to get it later.

Chapter Twenty-eight

By two AM the den had a cozier feel to it. The Monopoly money had established a relaxed tone right from the start, but the fine tuning came from the added touches. Guitars, socks, plates, popcorn kernels, uneaten crusts in a pizza box, two swimming noodles, and a growing, carefully stacked pyramid of iced tea tins on the coffee table, all made their own special contribution.

Darryl had one of the boxes the tea tins had come in on his head, watching a DVD through the handle slot punched in one end. Somewhere around midnight, he'd substituted it for his toque. The resemblance to a knight's jousting helmet had been immediately apparent, which explained why Sam had dug the swimming noodle lances out of the basement. Their current project was to drink their way through the second box. Then Sam would have a helmet, too, and the tournament could begin.

He was just beginning to think this phase of the project might have to wait until tomorrow, when the phone rang. After three rings, Sam located the phone in one of the guitar cases. Martha's hushed voice said, "What are you doing?"

Sam was surprised. He was also aroused. It was a very sexy voice. Unfortunately, he did not have a sexy answer. "Watching *Slime VII* with Darryl. Where are you?" He moved into the hallway as he spoke.

"In Quebec. We have, like, this little chalet. I have to keep quiet so Judy doesn't hear; she's still up. My mom zonked out ages ago. Too much vino with dinner."

"Won't she find out anyway?"

"How?"

"Well ..." It seemed to Sam that hotels charged you for telephone calls. He thought he remembered this from a school band trip to Montreal, where Darryl had claimed to have Johnny Depp's home phone number, downloaded from the Internet. It also seemed too late to go into this now, and maybe little chalets were different. "I dunno."

"Who cares if she does?" Martha said. "So, are you thinking of me?"

"Oh, yeah," Sam said.

"That's good. I'm thinking of you. God, it's such a drag up here. I wish my dad could've got time off to take me somewhere. At least I brought some weed."

"Well, I wish you were here," said Sam, keeping his voice low.

"Really? What would we do?"

It felt as if the phone was melting in his hand. "Well," he whispered so Darryl wouldn't hear, "*I'd* be looking for your tattoo again." Lately, they had both found this to be a diverting pastime.

Martha giggled. This seemed to have been the right answer. She whispered, "You'd have to look someplace you never have before."

"Hmm. Like where?"

"Oh, shit, Judy's coming. I gotta go. Bye."

The line went dead. Sam swallowed as he lowered the handset, then adjusted his boxers, which now felt cramped. Would this count as phone sex? What *would* they do if Martha were here? Or rather, what would they have the nerve to do? How far would they go? They'd gone pretty far, but not all the way. He walked back into the den. A greasy-looking five-hundred-dollar Monopoly bill stuck itself to his bare toe. He shook it; it didn't budge. He sagged onto the couch and ignored the problem. An uninterrupted evening with Martha would not involve Monopoly money, that was for sure. He wondered what Mrs. Gernsbach might recommend.

The DVD was on pause. From inside the iced tea carton Darryl said, "Was that Martha?"

"Huh?" Sam was startled. For a moment, he'd forgotten about Darryl. "Oh. Yeah." He pulled a cushion onto his lap until things calmed down.

"From Quebec? Sweet. Laura would never have done something like that."

Laura was a girl Darryl had gone out with in grade ten. It had been a tempestuous relationship that ended with Laura pouring a large drink into Darryl's lap as they watched a movie. Apparently he'd chosen the wrong place to rest his hand. Sam, sitting a few rows forward with everyone else, had watched Darryl's silhouette shoot straight up and block his view of the screen, just as the leader of the zombies jumped into the pool and grabbed the sexpot bad girl character who everyone knew was doomed from the second minute of the film. "Yeah," Darryl sighed, "there were a whole lot of things Laura wouldn't do."

Sam already knew. Darryl had not exactly been Mr. Discretion at the time. The box turned ever so slightly Sam's way.

"Does Martha, like ... do you ..."

"We do some things," Sam said cautiously.

"Is that, like, what you got in trouble about before Christmas?"

"No! Geez, Darryl, I didn't even meet Martha till after we went back to school."

He'd hoped Darryl would have forgotten pre-Christmas by now. He wondered if he was going to have to make something up, just to satisfy him.

But Darryl had already moved on. "Know what Amanda told me today?" As usual, he was more interested in whatever he wanted to say next. For once, Sam was relieved.

Darryl pushed the iced tea box up until his face was visible. "Laura's going out with this university guy, right? So she got mad at him and called him up so he could hear her hitting his mp3 player with a hammer."

"Really?" Sam asked.

"Yeah. Amanda heard it from Ashley, I think. She was there. Anyway, it was a little while ago." Darryl foraged in the popcorn bowl for stray edibles. He said, "It's not fair, you know? How come girls almost always go out with older guys?" He adjusted the box, which was slipping back down, and picked up one of the acoustic guitars. "I mean, what's the problem?" He slammed out a couple of chords. "Aren't we *mature* enough?"

Sam shrugged. He didn't want to discuss his own recent track record. On the other hand: "Well, we're mature enough to be here on our own, doing this."

"Yeah," said Darryl, vindicated. "And, like they're so mature? Right. Well, maturity is overrated." He bashed the chords again. And again. And again, until they settled into a da-da-da-da da-da-da-da rhythm. "Ma-tur-it-y is ov-er-rate-ed," he chanted. "It's like a punk song. It *is* a punk song! Okay, what rhymes with overrated?" With one hand, Darryl scrabbled up a pen from the coffee table and flipped over the pizza box. A crust and some crumbs tumbled out onto the carpet. "Double dated, operated ... c'mon, help me. We can do it at the next show in Toronto."

"Irritated," said Sam. "Constipated." He now held the other guitar. One of the things he liked about Darryl was that the guy was never down for long. And why should they be down? He'd done it; been mature. He'd pulled it off, and here they were, making out okay on their own, maturely discussing important questions, learning to drive, and writing a song to boot. So why was something niggling at him? He strummed a chord and a thought bubbled out: "You don't think Martha would smash anything, do you?"

"Martha? No, why?" Darryl kept scribbling. "How do you spell ovulated? Skip it."

"I dunno," Sam fumbled. "It's just, sometimes—"

"*Lotus would*," Darryl interrupted. "She creeps me out. What does Larry see in her? I mean, can you imagine—"

"Spare me," Sam nodded his agreement. "I bet he thought up going in the Leak race just 'cause he knew she'd want to."

"I thought it was you and Martha that had that idea."

"No way! I don't even want to go in the stupid thing."

"Why not? It'll be fun. Remember back when we did it in grade six? I'm glad we outgrew that. Animated!" Darryl scribbled again. "Anyway, I don't know who said it; we were all pretty impaired that night. Not as impaired as *you*, Chugger—"

"Yeah, yeah, yeah—"

"I just thought it was you 'cause you said you'd been in the store and everything."

"Well, we were."

Darryl looked up and his eyes narrowed. "Really?"

"Wait here."

Sam put down the guitar and hustled up to his room. His mother had taped a sign to his door reading COMPOSTABLE MATERIAL WITHIN. Usually he managed to ignore it. From the depths of his closet, he extracted a box in a now familiar bag, then returned to Darryl and tossed it on the couch.

"What is it?" Darryl asked. He put down the pen.

"Check it out."

Darryl popped open the box, spilling condom wrappers all over the couch. "Holy shit."

"From the store," Sam said.

Darryl was busy reading labels. "Ribbed. Day-glo. Peppermint Pleasure. Super Sense-o-Lite ... Man, you're set for life."

At his current rate of sexual intercourse, Sam knew, he was in fact set for eternity, even without the box. He avoided this by saying, "Yeah, except they're not for keeping. They're what we throw from the boat."

"Really?" said Darryl, holding one up. "So they weren't kidding about that. Hmm. Temptation Tickler. We gotta open this, just to see."

"Don't bother. I already checked."

"And?"

"Dead porcupine on a balloon."

"Oh." Darryl dropped the packet. Some of the others were already slipping between the cushions. He looked at them with clearly faked indifference.

"I heard somewhere," Sam said, "that we're supposed to think about sex once every six minutes."

"That's all?" said Darryl. He picked up a Peppermint Pleasure, which promised green day-glo striping for swirls of pleasure. "Just a souvenir."

Chapter Twenty-nine

"Let's get something to eat," Sam said as Darryl tucked the condom away. "Then I'm going to bed."

"What about the song?"

"We can think while we make sandwiches."

"Ah, yes, a last round of peanut butter sandwiches."

They headed to the kitchen, Darryl carting along the guitar and pizza box. Peanut butter and bread awaited them on the counter, along with many other important things.

"Toasted?"

"Toasted."

Strangely, the toaster, which had been fine earlier, was now not working.

"Do you think it was when you dropped it?" asked Darryl.

"I don't know; I didn't think it landed that hard. It *looks* okay."

"Damn," said Darryl. "I really wanted toast. Hey, *wait* a minute." Clearly it was Darryl's night for inspiration. He put down the guitar and pizza box. At the end of the counter, a clothes iron sat on its end, left over from some last-minute pressing Sam's mom had done as she packed. "Watch this," said Darryl. He plugged it in. Then he scooped a slice of bread from the loaf. After puzzling over the temperature dial, he twisted it, then lifted the iron and applied the bread to the bottom. "Brilliant, or what? Ah! Shit! You got an oven mitt thingy or anything?"

"No, wait," cried Sam, re-energized by Darryl's ingenuity. "Wait!"

He dashed to the linen closet and hauled out the spare iron. "Two at once!" He bustled back to the kitchen, plugged in, and moved close to Darryl, twisting the dial to high. "Okay, now, tilt yours down, so, like, the bread's in between."

"What? How? You mean like—"

"Watch your fingers—"

"Well, I can't—"

"No, wait; careful—"

"Ow—Yes!"

They faced each other, a slice of bread pinned between their irons.

"We should be at arm's length," said Darryl. "It would look more official."

Sam backed up. Crumbs crackled beneath his bare feet. He shook some out from between his toes. The Monopoly money was still there. "The Human Toast Machine."

"The Human *Iron* Toast Machine," Darryl corrected.

"The HIT Machine!"

"This is *so* cool."

A plume of smoke drifted upwards, accompanied by a burning smell. Darryl abruptly pulled his iron away. The blackened slice of bread dropped to the floor between them. "So it needs a little fine-tuning," he said.

By the second round each, it was agreed that HIT Machine sandwiches even tasted better. Granted, they took longer to make, and an experiment had shown it was definitely better to put the peanut butter on after ironing, but still. Sam sagely remembered to unplug the irons. Darryl licked his fingers. "What time is it?"

"Ten to three."

"First half-hour of *Armadillo*."

"Okay. We want to be fresh for the morning."

Chapter Thirty

By Wednesday morning, Sam felt as if he were in his own personal fog. He couldn't understand it; two mostly sleepless nights were almost more than he could handle. He was old before he'd even stopped being young. How did Keith Richards do it?

Standing at the kitchen counter, he poured the last of the cereal into a bowl that was passing for clean. Luckily, there was a spoon left in the drawer. A big one, for serving salad, but technically still a spoon. He stuck the end in the bowl, scattering sugared flakes of something across the counter. Several stuck to a knife handle coated in tomato sauce, one landed in the melted ice cream. One ticked against an iron, the bottom of which was enameled with baked-on peanut butter. A few others actually stayed on the giant spoon. Sam hoisted the dry cereal to his mouth and began to crunch. They'd run out of milk sometime Tuesday.

"You know what tastes good on those? Root beer." Darryl was at the table, having a cold hot dog for breakfast. Even if there had been bread, cranking up the HIT Machine would have been way too much trouble on three hours' sleep. In fact, almost everything was. Sam stopped chewing. The cereal tasted like sugar-coated wood chips. He contemplated having a glass of water, but that would have meant reaching over and turning on the tap. Besides, there were no clean glasses. Finally, he swallowed painfully and said, "We have to clean up after driving today."

Darryl nodded and teased the last hot dog from the pack.

"Shouldn't take long."

"I guess." Sam stepped over a sofa cushion. He'd used it for a shield during the previous evening's jousting. Out in the hall, he could see the light flashing on the answering machine. This roused a vague memory of his mom's voice buzzing from it sometime the night before. Since he and Darryl had been in the middle of a *Family Guy* retrospective and the phone had temporarily vanished, Sam had let it go at the time, the machine being way down by the front door. He decided to collect the message before they left, then saw that all the pictures below the stairs were askew, collateral damage from jousting. It had been hard to see out the holes of those iced tea boxes. He straightened one and felt better. "Anyway," he said, "my folks don't get back till after supper."

"We're laughing." Darryl's voice came from the den. It was followed by da-da-da-da da-da-da-da on a guitar. "Maturity is overrated," Darryl sang in the same rhythm. "I just masturbated ..." He had found his rhyme; in fact, the whole song was done. Wait till Larry heard it.

Driving lessons were not done. Shuffling through another bracing March morning, Sam came to long enough to realize he had no lunch money. Then he remembered he hadn't collected his mom's message, either. There'd be time when they were cleaning up.

Luckily, a short nap during the videos and a lunch financed by a small loan from Delft worked wonders. The fresh air helped, too. It was overcast as they trooped to Little Hope Variety at lunchtime, milder than earlier. Sam breathed deeply and caught an earthy tang in the wind. Something in him lifted with the breeze. In the past few days, he'd demonstrated Responsibility, Co-ordination, and Songwriting Ability. He had what it took to thrive after two parent-free days in a

Pants Optional Zone. How many could claim the same? He watched Darryl stumble straight through a puddle. Clearly, not many. And now, from this mountaintop of, yes, Maturity, he looked ahead to a happy drive, a quick house tidy, and a restful rest of spring break, basking in glory while his dad made dinners. (You could overdo the independence thing.) He bit joyfully into his pizza slice. Scattered drops of rain nibbled at the crusts of filthy snow around the parking lot, reminding him he was overdue for a shower. Yes, spring had truly come.

"All right," said Marvell, as they gathered by the car after lunch. "Sam the Man, you're kicking off, then Delft, then Darryl. It's backfield in motion today, people: three-point turns and parallel parking."

Remembering to do everything correctly, including start the car, Sam followed Marvell's directions and drove them a few blocks to a quiet side street the Fosters sometimes took as a back way to the grocery store. It hardly mattered, Sam thought; the whole town was a quiet side street. Marvell coached him through a couple of three-point turns. They were a breeze.

Then, "Pull over," Marvell said. He got out of the car and extracted some orange traffic cones from the trunk, which he used to mark a rectangle by the curb. The compact groaned as he got back in. "Now," Marvell said, "that's a car you have to parallel park behind. Make sure the street is clear, then pull up beside it."

Sam did as he was told. As the car idled, Marvell went over the steps for parallel parking. It seemed simple enough: Back up; cut the wheel as the door passed the rear pylon; don't hit the pylons; and don't hit the curb.

"I'm not gonna ride my brake," the big man said. "So get in the zone.

Be aware of your space. You have to *live* the car, all right? Sense it; it's an extension of you."

Sam nodded as if he understood this.

"Let's go."

On his first try, he clipped a pylon. On his second, he slid the car into its spot. Marvell opened the passenger door. They were a good three feet from the curb. "Double extra-large," he said. "My old size. Better and better, my man. One more try. You're gonna nail it this time."

Sam breathed deeply. He *was* going to nail it this time. Rain spattered the windshield, reminding him again of that shower. It was important to be on top of these things. They were part of being Mature and Responsible. Speaking of which, he was going to have to collect that message, too. As long as it wasn't about getting something from the store, it would be fine. He was out of money. But enough of that now. He shook off petty concerns; it was time to ace parallel parking.

He looked to Marvell, who nodded. He casually set the windshield wipers to intermittent, avoiding Darryl's sorry Tuesday mistake of twisting the cigarette lighter. Then he flicked on the left-turn signal and put the car in gear. Checking his mirrors, he waited for a green Honda van, just like the Fosters' own, to roll by. The road was clear. He pulled out and up beside the orange cones. On went the right-turn signal.

"Looking good," murmured Marvell. "We clear?"

Sam checked his mirror, then glanced ahead. The road was empty, except for the van, slowing for the stop sign at the end of the block. It, too, had a right turn signal flashing.

"Now," Marvell was saying, "ease it back."

Sam put the car in reverse and looked over his shoulder, then eased up on the brake. The car began a slow roll back.

"Now cut the wheel ... a little more ..."

Sam risked a glance ahead to make sure he was going to clear the pylons. His wiper blade swept the windshield clear and Sam had a sudden, crystalline view of the green van as it turned. His mom was framed in the passenger window.

"AHH!" Sam said. His foot slammed to the floor. The car shot back. Everyone screamed. There was a bone-rattling jolt, then a long, grinding vibration, and the rear of the car lifted off, jerking everyone forward against their safety belts until, at an impossible, about-to-flip-over-teetering-on-the-front-bumper angle, they stopped.

Hanging breathlessly, Sam fought down a remix of pizza and chocolate milk. The air was filled with a whining roar. Over the noise Marvell said, "Take your foot off the gas."

Sam did as he was told. The roaring faded. The wiper blade passed again. They were looking, dizzyingly, almost straight down at some icy grit on a yellow lawn. It was like a horrible parody of a theme park ride, except there was no attendant to help you out.

"What happened?" Darryl's voice quavered from the back seat.

"He backed us up one of those cables that hold the telephone poles." Delft sounded stunned.

"I have never seen that before," Marvell said thoughtfully.

"How do we get out of here?" Darryl demanded.

"We seem to be balanced," Marvell said. "Let's just sit nice and still while I call for a little help on my cell, here, and then we'll see if we can't figure something out. No rush, now; let's just take it slow and easy."

Sam rested his forehead on the steering wheel. The *deet deet*

deet of Marvell punching numbers into his cell phone sounded beside him. No rush, indeed. His parents ought to be opening the front door to Hell any minute now. With twenty-twenty hindsight, he guessed that the uncollected phone message was his mom warning him they'd be home early. It had been a fast trip down Maturity Mountain, all the way to rock bottom.

Darryl said, "Hey, here comes someone from that house. Maybe he can help us."

"Oh, my God," said Delft. "It's Mr. Tegwar."

Rock bottom clearly had a basement.

Part Four

BOTTOM

Chapter Thirty-one

"Like it?" Martha asked.

Sam unfolded the τ-shirt she'd brought him. Printed on it was: *Your village called: Their idiot is missing.*

"Great," Sam said. Actually, it cut a little close to the bone after spring break. "I'll wear it tomorrow." He bent to give her a quick kiss, then tucked the shirt under his arm and took another bite of sandwich. Like most of the students at Hope Springs High, they were strolling the halls at lunch on this first Monday back at school. It was also Sam's first chance to see Martha since her return. She had a new shirt, too; it read REHAB IS FOR QUITTERS.

Martha looked in her lunch bag but didn't take anything out. She was also clutching a paperback copy of *Rule of the Bone*. "You've gotta read this," she said. "Mrs. Stephens showed it to me. Get it out soon as I'm done, okay?"

"Okay." Sam was between books right now. You had a lot of time to read when you were grounded on spring break.

"So, you're not grounded anymore?" Martha asked.

"No, but I might be if they ever notice the microwave." The CD had melted so smoothly and evenly that you could barely see it on the revolving glass tray. This made it different from the baked peanut-butter finish on the spare iron. Of course, that would have been harder to see if he hadn't left all the lights on. "But I've got to work in the store for free for every hour it took to clean the house. And ace all my assignments. *And* I can't do my driver's test until I prove I'm more responsible. And my mom isn't too crazy about the crazy craft, so that's not helping."

"I'll sweet-talk her," Martha assured him. "Don't worry. We need you if we're going to get the boat done. And you're going to get the condoms back, right?"

"Oh, yeah." The condoms scattered around the family room had been easier to deal with than anything else, thanks to the Leak race. Still, Sam's mom had been less than thrilled by what she'd heard. "Tasteless" and "stupid" had been her adjectives, actually.

"Does Mrs. Gernsbach know about this?" she'd asked, gathering up little plastic packets before vacuuming. Sam was helping. His mom's eyes had narrowed. "Because she's got enough people hassling her now, without you stirring things up. Understand?"

"I understand," Sam had nodded as he felt around under the couch cushions.

"I hope so. Because I thought you understood mature behavior before we went away."

"We would have cleaned up! I just didn't get your message."

"Oh? It was on the machine. Sam, mature behavior also includes *bothering* to collect phone messages that might be important. You're in charge when we're not around. What if I'd needed your help and was trying to contact you?"

"You'd have called back?"

A silence had followed as his mom stared at him. Then, "Plug in the vacuum. And why is there a swimming noodle behind the couch?"

Now, as they passed into the main foyer of the school, Sam was starting to feel like that guy from myths in grade nine, who had to keep pushing a rock up a hill and every time, it would roll back down. Pre-Christmas, Baby Tegbun, the Valentine's dance, and now this: When was he going to catch a break? To make matters worse, he remembered: "We've got *Amazings* rehearsals, too."

"Gawd, I know. Listen, I'm going out for a butt; then I've gotta go beg for an extension for my history."

"Didn't you do it?"

"Dream on; I wasn't wasting March Break on that crap. Anyway, how could I? I was *away*, remember? Don't worry; Jones is a pushover. I'll see you in ten, okay? At your locker. Gawd."

Martha threw her uneaten lunch into a garbage can and headed, coatless, for the front doors. Sam started upstairs. Mrs. Goldenrod was coming down.

"Sam," she called, "don't forget: meeting tomorrow night."

"Okay." Sam nodded politely instead of groaning aloud. He had had to field several J. Earl committee calls last week; while he sat home evenings, and he'd felt like an idiot because he couldn't answer a single question anyone had asked. He felt even dumber now that he remembered he hadn't written any of the questions down, either—except for one, and it had washed off in the shower.

Thank God Mrs. Goodenough had gotten back home on the weekend. On Friday, Marvell had said J. Earl was going a little stir crazy. "Mr. Work-In-Progress," Marvell had shaken his head, "but he can't read the dial on the washing machine. Or the dishwasher. Man, I've been in fresher *locker* rooms."

He passed through the doors at the top of the stairs to an

unpleasantly familiar sound: the wail of a computerized doll. Amanda was fumbling with her books and the key-on-a-bracelet all at once. Delft looked on sympathetically; Baby Bunteg's replacement had arrived.

"See you at *Amazings*," he called to Delft, and kept moving. Down by Mrs. Goldenrod's room, Darryl was energetically acting something out to a small audience. He shot up on his toes, pitched forward, and stuck his butt in the air. Clearly today's performance was *How Sam Balanced a Car on Its Front Bumper*. So much for Chugger. He turned back, only to meet his dad and Mr. Tegwar, strolling toward him, chatting. The Teginator, who rose as high as Mr. Foster's shoulder, was wearing a bow tie, the only thing that could have made him look even less fashionable.

"After school," reminded Mr. Foster, the director. "Music room."

Sam nodded again. Before he could move on, Mr. Tegwar said, "Yes, I'm ... uh ... looking forward to that myself."

Sam nodded yet again. Mr. Tegwar cleared his throat. "I trust that the rest of your driver training wasn't as ... uh ... *bumpy*."

"Oh, yes. I mean, no." The rest of driver training had been mercifully uneventful. Marvell had somehow explained away the accident and Sam had gotten his certificate. "Sorry about your lawn."

"That part is town property," said Mr. Tegwar. "And with everything still frozen, there was not much damage."

Sam wished he could say the same about the car.

"You were rather nose-to-the-curbstone and shoulder-on-the-wheel." Mr. Tegwar smiled primly. Mr. Foster laughed at what Sam figured was some kind of joke. He didn't get it, but he smiled to show he did.

Mr. Foster said, "Oh, yeah, he was *hanging* in there."

Now it was Mr. Tegwar's turn to look puzzled. Then, "Oh, yes ... ehn-ehn-ehn." This, apparently was the sound of Tegwarian laughter. Sam had never heard it before. It seemed like the appropriate soundtrack to a day where every dumb move of his life was on rerun for everyone's pleasure.

As the adults headed off, Martha reappeared, scudding down the hall like a storm cloud. Oh-oh, Sam thought.

"Shithead Jones gave me zero," she snapped.

"Zero?"

"Said he'd already warned me: no extensions, no excuses. So now I'm going to fail the course. I mean, what does he want? I go to class, don't I? I *participate*. Shi-i-it. So that's math and history screwed. What an asshole."

"Oh, man ..."

"Know what? I don't care anyway. It's all bullshit. What'd numbnuts want?" She jerked her head in the direction of Mr. Tegwar.

"I think he was trying to be nice," Sam said.

Chapter Thirty-two

After school, Sam, Delft, and Darryl trooped dutifully to the music room, where they joined everyone else involved in the Hope Springs High School production of *The Amazings*. Or everyone but Martha. She hadn't been at her locker after last class, which probably meant she'd skipped. His dad didn't like it when people skipped rehearsal. He said it was inconsiderate. Maybe it was just as well, though, Sam thought. He hadn't wanted to witness his father trying to direct Martha when she was pissed off. Nobody told Martha anything when she was pissed off. Actually, Sam didn't really want to witness his father trying to direct a play at all, so he was relieved when most of the cast went next door to the drama room, to run scenes. The musicians would remain behind to begin working on songs with the soloists.

Mr. Carnoostie seated himself at the electric keyboard. Sam settled himself behind the school's drum kit. The others organized chairs and music stands.

"I thought we'd start with the signature tune," said Mr. Carnoostie. "It's the only one anyone ever remembers, and, sooner or later, just about everyone reprises it. So, 'Flickering Candles,' instrumental version. Then we'll get Delft in to sing it."

Everyone shuffled through their scores. Mr. Tegwar clamped his reed between his lips to wet it. He looked vaguely like a gray-haired Baby Teggy with a soother and a bow tie. Sam felt himself relax for the first time all day. With no ADHD practice, he hadn't been playing much at all; he hadn't realized how much he'd missed it. And, except for Mr. Tegwar, everyone here had been in Maple Nitro. Mr. Carnoostie played through the intro to the song. Sam counted bars, came in on three with the brushes, and they were off. It was a simple, lilting waltz. The clarinet took the melody. Mr. Tegwar played a little stiffly, but with a clear tone that warmed and rounded the second time through.

"Bitchin' horn," complimented Mr. Gernsbach when they finished, proving that he had indeed gone to high school in the early 1960s. "With those glasses, you even look like Benny Goodman."

"Well ... uh ... goodness, thank you." Mr. Tegwar offered his second smile of the day, a record.

"Sam," called Mr. Carnoostie, "would you go and get Delft, please?"

Sam walked to the drama room. He was startled to see that his dad was blocking out a scene with Martha and two others. When had she arrived? He tapped Delft on the shoulder. "It's that time."

As they walked back, Sam noticed for the first time that Delft had been letting her hair grow longer. How long had she been doing that, he wondered? In profile, she now looked like ... well, someone else. Then he remembered: Back in their Maple Nitro days, her dad had her do a country karaoke act in disguise as "Madison Dakota," complete with a long wig. Which meant she now actually looked like herself. Again. Or rather, she looked like Madison Dakota. Sam had liked Madison Dakota. He said, "Hey, your hair is different. It's like ..." Then he paused, remembering Delft had not liked Madison Dakota.

"I know," she said. "Like my old wig. Do *you* like it? I'm not sure." Before he could work out an answer, Delft asked, "Is Mr. Tegwar in there?"

"Yeah, but he's good. I was stunned."

"Really? God, he makes me nervous. I hope I can sing."

There was no time to answer this, either. They were back at the music room.

"So, Delft," grinned Mr. Carnoostie, "'Flickering Candles.' We've got an eight-bar intro and you're in. Okay? Need the lyrics?"

Delft shook her head. Her new hair stirred. Sam saw her glance uncertainly at Mr. Tegwar and turn slightly away from him. He did have that effect on people. Behind the drums, Sam gave her an encouraging smile. The intro began.

Nerves or not, Delft sang. With lessons, her voice had gotten even better over the last two years. This time, with Mr. Tegwar's clarinet filling the spaces around the vocal, the waltz had a mellow lilt to it that let you hear how it had become a hit. They ran through the song again, just because everyone liked it so much. Then they tried Delft's solo spot, called "I Wish." The melody was a yawner, but the vocal was not. This time, Mr. Tegwar's clarinet was plaintive, alone before a wash of brushes and a touch of Mr. Gernsbach's bass. There was no doubt about it. The man could play.

"Super!" enthused Mr. Carnoostie, his round cheeks glowing. "Gee, I wish it could all sound like that. Thanks, Delft. Could you send in Zack and Trevor, please?"

Delft flashed a quick smile at Sam and ducked out. He was still glowing from the music when Zack and Trevor shambled in. They played the tyrannical fathers, though in hip-hop and hard-core jeans respectively, they left a lot to the imagination. As singers, they left a lot to the imagination also. "Flickering Candles" almost flickered out. They seemed to know this, because Zack said, "We're better on our own song."

This was a number called "Brussels Sprouts, I've Got My Doubts," a duet in which the two dads, in adjacent back yards, fumed over the elopement of their kids. The song was lame, though Sam liked his part, which featured thumps and crashes on odd beats, especially near the end. Zack and Trevor were lamer.

"It's better with the actions," said Zack.

They tried it again. Zack pretended to trim maniacally with nonexistent garden shears. Trevor mimed picking vegetables. The actions did distract from the bad singing. Then Trevor went one better. Bending low for an invisible veggie, he split the seat of his skin-tight jeans. "Stink!" cried Trevor, being a non-swearing Christian hard-core.

"Can we put that in the show?" Darryl wondered.

"It's better with the props," Zack said.

By five-thirty, Sam was cautiously driving his dad and Darryl home. Martha had refused a ride.

"I bet Trevor was wearing girl's jeans," Darryl said from the back seat of the van.

Sam didn't answer, giving his all to the driving. He found himself constantly on the lookout for hydro poles and cables. Despite his certificate, he felt less than confident. Waiting to take his driver's test was, secretly, just fine with him.

"So that's why he did the rest of the rehearsal in a trench coat," said Mr. Foster. "Well, that's about the only thing I saw today that doesn't need straightening out."

Mr. Foster remained deep in thought all the rest of the way home. When they finally arrived, a message to call the Goodenoughs awaited Sam. He called.

Mrs. Goodenough answered. "Sam!" she growled in her whiskey-and-cigarettes voice. She sounded tired. "Thanks for calling back. Do something for me, kiddo. When you go to that meeting tomorrow night, tell them that no matter what they've heard, Earl is fine. He just had to go into hospital for some routine tests. And if anyone wants to know more, he says to tell them he's having a nasal depilatory procedure."

Chapter Thirty-three

When Sam sat down to dinner the next evening, there were two candy-striped condom packets at his place setting. "They were in the refrigerator," his mom said. "I'm not even asking. I'm assuming you'll need them for the Leak race—and nothing else."

Sam felt himself blushing over his plate of Lentils Supreme. "Oh. Yeah. Thanks."

"Are you guys ready?" Mr. Foster served himself. "You could be the highlight."

Sam made a noncommittal noise around the French bread he was chewing. He tended to eat a lot of bread when Lentils Supreme was for supper. Conversation avoidance was harder now that Robin was back at school, and this was a sensitive topic.

"I don't think highlight is the word," Mrs. Foster said. "It's a family event. Did you find out if Mrs. Gernsbach knows what you have planned?"

Having finally swallowed, Sam was forced to answer.

"I don't know. I forgot to ask Martha." This was not exactly true, but safer all round than saying, "I didn't want to ask Martha." And he didn't plan to ask Martha any potentially upsetting questions until she cooled down about her history ISU.

"Well, you'd better ask her. And if you don't, I will, the next time I see her. Mrs. Gernsbach doesn't need any more headaches right now." She stirred her Lentils Supreme but didn't eat. Sam had a sudden hunch she didn't like it any more than he did. "At the last DBA meeting, we got a petition for a ban on main street businesses that 'contribute to an unwholesome image for the community.'" The DBA was the Downtown Business Association. This year, Mrs. Foster was chairperson.

Mr. Foster, who was eating heartily, snorted. "The only obscene things downtown are some of the prices. Who in the world would crank up an 'unwholesome image' petition?"

"I'll give you one guess."

Mr. Foster forked up more lentils. "Felice Doberman."

"Bingo. Remember when she had speakers put outside to play Mozart, just to drive kids away?"

Sam remembered. He also knew which kids at school were responsible for repeatedly vandalizing the speakers. This was not information he had shared. Meanwhile, his mom was saying, "She always has to run everything."

Sam interrupted. "Is that why she's on the J. Earl committee? I mean, she's at war with Mrs. Goldenrod, and she doesn't even like J. Earl."

"Bingo."

"Hey," said Mr. Foster, "that's not the only reason. You told me."

Mrs. Foster rolled her eyes and chuckled. "Okay. Sam, here's a little not-so-secret that you wouldn't know. Mrs. Doberman and Mrs. Goldenrod were both after J. Earl years ago. They were both single sweet young things—well, Elvira Goldenrod was married, but her hubby had already floated away after a three-day acid trip; she was a real hippy chick, you know—and J. Earl was older and already well-known. J. Earl was quite the ladies' man, back when he had hair. The girl who became Mrs. Doberman was not happy when J. Earl cut her loose."

"But Mrs. Goldenrod didn't get him, either."

"Doesn't matter; she's not letting her old rival run the show. Besides, now that she and Mr. Doberman have split, who knows what she's thinking?"

"Oh, man." Sam fought down his gag reflex. This was definitely too much information. Old-people sex was almost as bad as *parent* old-people sex—which reminded him of the bag he'd found in his parents' room at March Break. He felt his skin crawl. But then, his mom was talking about these people when they had been young. Okay, not young, but youngish; in their twenties, maybe, which would have made them middle-aged. J. Earl, though, would still have been a geezer in his forties. He envisioned Mrs. Goldenrod and Mrs. Doberman in mini-dresses and beads. It was not a happy thought. "I can't believe—"

"Felice Doberman was a hottie when she was young? Sam, she's still a very attractive woman now. Back then, her summer job was slinging beer in the Hope Haven Hotel. She used to wear a man's suit vest with nothing under it."

"How do you know?" Mr. Foster teased. He had not grown up in Hope Springs. "Were you sneaking in under age?"

"Never mind," Mrs. Foster said. "Everyone knew everything about everybody. J. Earl was a regular there, too."

"But, they're so ... so—"

"Old? For crying out loud, Sam. They weren't always."

"Always?" said Mr. Foster indignantly. "Except for J. Earl, they're not even old now. They're only in their fifties, for God's sake." Mr. Foster himself was forty-nine. Sam wondered if he was feeling the heat a little himself. Charitably, he decided not to mention that being in your fifties was the same as being six hundred and twelve. He tried not to look at his plate. All this talk had left him grossed-out enough, and he still had the J. Earl meeting to come.

Chapter Thirty-four

With dinner finished, Sam brushed his teeth and went to get his coat. His dad, waiting at the door, tossed him the car keys. Sam winced. "Again?"

"Again," said Mr. Foster. "You need to get your confidence back."

It was mild for the end of March. They climbed in the van. Sam began his rituals of mirror and seatbelt; his dad slouched in the passenger seat, watching. "Take your time."

They inched out of the driveway and down the street. Sam began braking well before the stop sign.

"There's nothing wrong with a little caution," Mr. Foster said, "but ... uh ... don't make yourself late. How are the music rehearsals coming?"

"Fine." Sam looked both ways. He didn't want to talk right now. He eased them through the intersection.

"Yup, a little caution. Shows you're learning. That's not always a bad thing."

Sam braked for a crosswalk. There was no one there, but you never knew.

"It's a delicate balance," his dad went on. "Sometimes in rehearsal I want everyone to just go for it, you know? Stop being so cautious. But then you need to think, too; to listen and learn ..."

Sam had heard all this before, every time his dad did a school play. It made a comforting background hum as they drove. At ten kilometers an hour he could almost feel every pebble beneath the tires, especially when he gripped the steering wheel this hard. Or was that the feel of his fingernails digging into his palms? Whatever. It was good; it felt like control.

"Of course," Mr. Foster was saying, "the real problem is when actors think they're being daring and they're not. Sometimes the real risk is in underplaying. It takes a long time to learn that outrageous can be boring."

This, too, was a rerun. Another stop sign loomed. Sam flicked his left-turn signal and braked. Three blocks away, a car was approaching. He waited for it to go by, just in case. It took a while. Still, you never could tell and, fortunately, no one was behind him. In the silence broken only by the clicking of the turn signal, his dad said, "Martha, for example can be rather independent-minded."

Normally, this would have tripped Sam's Coded Adult Message sensors, but the comment came as the oncoming car finally passed and he locked into his turn. Besides, the next thing his dad said was, "Sam, an old lady on a scooter is passing us."

He looked out the window. Over on the sidewalk, Mrs. Kipling, the Tourette's lady, was neck-and-neck with them. He picked up the pace, a little.

By the time Sam angled into a parking space, his dad's knees were bouncing and he was drumming his fingers on the door panel. "I'll be back at eight," Mr. Foster sighed. "Happy meetings."

Sam got to the library door just ahead of Mrs. Kipling, who smiled and offered an assortment of gestures and obscenities in return for his greeting. Inside, he slouched past the desk, toward the meeting room. Over at one of the computers he saw a head of green hair. He'd have to say hi later; his dad had been right about the time.

Luckily, he wasn't the only one late: Mrs. Stephens and Mrs. Doberman still hadn't arrived. He looked for a moment at Mrs. Goldenrod, dressed casually tonight in faded jeans and a sweatshirt featuring the face of a severe-looking woman with a squint. Still standing, she hefted her tote bag to the table and bent to find something inside. For an instant, her hair clung to the arc of her neck. It looked girlish, hinting at the flower-child that had been. Sam found it an oddly sexy moment. Then she looked up and was Mrs. Goldenrod again.

Sam stepped from the room. If there was still time, he felt like surprising Martha by hustling her off for a quick kiss in the stacks. She'd never expect that.

Martha wasn't at the computer. Perhaps she was in the washroom. Her coat was still slung over the chair back, with *Rule of the Bone* and some papers artfully arranged on the table to suggest homework-in-progress. Sam had plenty himself back at home.

Still, homework wasn't Martha's style, was it? He bent to look at the computer screen. He was right, she was on MSN again, to Lotus, he'd bet. Feeling only slightly guilty, he peered in to see what they were talking about.

> ... bossing us around like hes king shit. lol. i almost told him screw you he thinks hes so coolso ilooked at him and said really loud SCREW—and then waited a sec and was like —ups can happen you know. then he goes all red but he cant say anything right so finally he goes yeah but all quiet then he talks to someone

else. god i dont even know why im doing this its so stupid. i should reck it but then maybe sam would get in trouble

»»ɛÐ⁺ûš° says:
what u have to do is make it so that it looks like the ZOTFL wrecked it. That would be so cool haha hed probably crap his surfer shorts

º*må°+ha*'º says:
LOL Wait till they see the SECRET WEAPON on the boat. the whole town will crap my dad will love it hes coming down. brb high times. u still have 2 tell me about u and hswlarry... u kno...??? HEY im getting the pill too.

Sam straightened up and backed away from the computer table, feeling crooked inside. Martha was still nowhere to be seen. Smitty was waving to him from the meeting room. He let Mrs. Kipling roll by, then headed back as fast as he could.

Chapter Thirty-five

Everyone except Mrs. Doberman was now present.

"I know we're all busy, so let's start, just this once," said Mrs. Goldenrod happily. "After all, we only have a couple of weeks left." The severe lady on her chest squinted back at them unevenly, one eye retreating and her long nose accentuated by the ripple and bulge of the sweatshirt. In the midst of his turmoil over what he'd just read, Sam startled himself by noticing for the first time that Mrs. Goldenrod had quite large breasts; in fact, a major rack. He surprised himself further by imagining them beneath her sweatshirt. What was she wearing? As he riffled through his imagination's bra file, he suddenly realized he was being asked a question.

"How is J. Earl? I heard that he was unwell."

"I ... what? Oh, that." Sam fought for clarity. He could feel himself beginning to blush. "No ... uh ... he's fine. Mrs. Goodenough told me it was just a regular thing. She said he had to have this naval depilatory proceeding? I mean, procedure."

Eyebrows went up around the table, including, it seemed, the severe lady's, who then seemed to go cross-eyed. Some confused discussion ensued. Sam tried not to think about nipples. Once every six minutes? Forget it.

"Naval or navel?"

"Well, he was in the Navy."

"Wait," Sam corrected. "I think she said it was nasal."

"He was having hairs removed from his nose?"

"Say, listen," said an older man across the table, "it can be quite a problem. My barber was telling me about a guy couldn't get fitted for a hearing aid he had so much hair in his ears."

"But, my God, you just use the nail scissors—"

"Well, I think—"

Sam improvised before he could be grilled for more details. "Actually, I think that was a joke. You know you said he was in the Navy? He was having a tattoo removed."

"Go on!"

"Well, I never!"

That J. Earl! Except for Mrs. Goldenrod and the severe lady, who both gave him a calculating look, everyone was chuckling. The topic had been defused. Sam figured it hadn't been the smoothest lie he'd ever told, but it seemed to have done the trick, just the way Mrs. Goodenough had wanted. Mrs. Goldenrod broke off her look, the severe lady settled back over her breasts, and they both turned to Smitty with a question about volunteer helpers.

Sam then parried a request that he do a presentation on behalf of youth at the gala evening by reminding everyone that he'd be busy at the opening of the school musical that night. His confidence was seeping back, mingling with the sour undercurrent of Martha's MSN script. And she'd said she was getting the pill, too. Wait a minute. Did that mean THE pill? Which would mean she wanted to … with …

He was interrupted by Mrs. Doberman's noisy arrival. "You shouldn't have waited," she announced, bustling in. Her face was flushed. She dumped her purse and binder on the table, then shrugged off her fur coat and attempted to drape it over the back of her chair. It slid to the floor. She didn't seem to notice.

"Sorry I'm late," said Mrs. Doberman. "Iss just bin one thing after." Sam saw that she, too, was in jeans, but topped with a pricey-looking ski sweater and a pair of half-glasses on a finder string. She stumbled slightly and saw her coat on the floor. As she bent to retrieve it, something else became apparent: Mrs. Doberman had a sensational ass. In fact she was a ... gulp ... MILF. Sam was stunned: His mom had been right. Why had he never noticed this before? He felt his face burning. Between Mrs. Doberman's butt and Mrs. Goldenrod's chest, there didn't seem to be a safe place to look. What was going on with him tonight? What was going on with everyone?

"Phew." Mrs. Doberman's nether assets disappeared as she plopped into her chair and fumbled with her meeting gear. A pen skittered across the table. She muttered something that could have been, "Shit," and snaked out a hand to retrieve it, bumping Mrs. Stephens's LIBRARY LOVERS DO IT QUIETLY mug. Tea sloshed. Mrs. Doberman began to hum what Sam recognized as the riff from Led Zeppelin's "Whole Lotta Love." Her head bobbed to the beat as she shuffled her papers. Sam looked at Smitty. Smitty shot him back a look. He was barely keeping a straight face.

"Actually, Felice," said Mrs. Stephens, calmly sopping up the tea with some tissues, "we were just discussing protocol for some of the gala guests."

Mrs. Doberman mustn't have heard, because she drawled, "Al-l-l-l-l-l ..." and then, after an excruciatingly long pause, "... Ri-i-i-i-ight. Naaow ... first thing I need to know, is Earl coming to any of the pub nights?"

Her head snapped up. The room went dead at this question from left field. Mrs. Doberman was clearly not herself tonight, though what she had become, apart from a Yummy Mummy, was a mystery to Sam. Now he found himself in her slightly wavering sights as she waited for someone to answer. Nonsensically, it occurred to him that if Mrs. Goldenrod had the glasses dangling around her neck, it would look as if the severe lady was wearing them. Or Mrs. Goldenrod's breasts. He shifted uncomfortably. When was she going to look away? He willed someone to answer the question. Instead, the silence deepened. Finally, still staring at him, Mrs. Doberman said, "Well, what did he *sayyyy*?"

Sam stared back helplessly. How would he know? Then he flinched. This was one of the phone call questions he hadn't done anything about. "Uh ... well ... he said it kind of depends on his leg."

"I guess the tattoo won't be a problem by then," someone else said.

"Depends where he gets it removed from," someone else kidded. Mrs. Doberman's penciled eyebrows knitted, then arched as she followed this.

Sam cut in with, "We probably need to ask his physiotherapist if he's up to it."

Across the table, Mrs. Doberman's eyebrows settled into a leer.

"Mr. Byrd? I'd *love* to ask him exactly that."

There was nervous chuckling around the table. She burped. "Pard. Well, we need to know. The pub nights are important. I mean," and here she gave a kind of giggling snort, "he nearly used to live in them. Of course, in those days, *he* was up to it."

"Oh, that's not true." Heads swiveled. Mrs. Goldenrod was glaring; she'd pulled herself ramrod straight, causing the severe lady to swell noticeably. Sam felt an unmistakable pang of lust. Mrs. Doberman, on the other hand, looked back with slack-jawed disdain.

"Oh, spare me, Elvira. He wasn't Goody Two Shoes and we both know it. Why don't you bogart one like *you* used to and just mellow out?"

The room went silent. Sam was riveted.

"You're drunk," snapped Mrs. Goldenrod, the color in her face rising with her voice. "And for your information, I never bogarted—unlike some people."

"Well, I didn't have time. I was too busy with Earl."

"Too busy. Ha. Looking for his tattoo."

"He doesn't have a tattoo."

"That's what you think. But that's all it was for you, wasn't it? You never appreciated his mind!"

"Well, *you* didn't even have one, with a head full of MDA—"

Their fascinating exchange was interrupted by a high-pitched burst of obscenities from the library. Then came a heart-stopping crash. Everybody started. Smitty and Mrs. Stephens were the first to move; Sam crowded out behind them as the others followed.

March air was swirling through the reading room, rippling papers and the leaves of the potted palms. Astonished patrons stood staring at the back wall, where one of the floor-to-ceiling windows had vanished. Outside, a jumble of shapes flailed in the shadows. There was a good deal more yelling. A cone of light fluttered close to the ground like a deranged moth.

Sam followed Smitty and Mrs. Stephens through the gaping hole where the window had been. Granulated glass scritched beneath his feet. Mrs. Kipling was still astride her scooter, which she had apparently driven straight through the window.

"Sorry," she panted, her ticcing momentarily banished. "I was so surprised."

Pinned beneath a bush by the vehicle, a struggling figure lay on the ground, clutching a flashlight. For once, the light was not illuminating the flasher's private parts. "My ankle," gasped the flasher, "my ankle." It was a familiar voice. Sam looked closer and felt himself do something he'd only seen in movies: a double take. On the ground lay Mr. Tegwar.

Chapter Thirty-six

There was something about a surprise test comparing tragic archetypes in *Macbeth* and *The Great Gatsby* that struck Sam as unfair for a Friday afternoon. Even Family Studies would have been better. Mrs. Goldenrod collected the papers just before the bell rang. Despite it being a dress-down day, she was wearing a no-nonsense skirt and sweater. Since the uproar at the library, it was almost as if she'd gone out of her way to look as unsexy as possible—not that she'd been a hottie before, excepting that odd moment or two in the meeting. "Have a nice weekend," she said.

Have a nice weekend. Sam levered himself out of his seat, feeling drained. The past ten days had been a nonstop grind of mid-terms, ISUs, rehearsals, crazy craft building, and decisions, and it wasn't over yet. Tomorrow was the Leak race, followed by a full run-through of *The Amazings*. Hope For J. Earl week started on Monday, the play opened Thursday, *and* ADHD had to find time for a practice because their May show was just around the corner.

As they all shuffled to the door, Delft asked, "Did anybody say Myrtle was the Lady Macbeth of *Gatsby*?"

"Uh-huh," said Larry.

Myrtle was Lady Macbeth? Oh-oh. Sam hadn't even thought about Myrtle. He decided not to say anything. This was a choice he'd been making a lot lately. For example, apart from his parents, he hadn't told anyone about the meltdown between Mrs. Goldenrod and Mrs. Doberman.

His parents were also the only people he'd told about Mr. Tegwar. Martha had been long gone when it happened. The teacher had remained pinned on a patch of ice in the bushes until the police and ambulance arrived. At school, it had been announced that Mr. Tegwar was away on medical leave. Even so, all kinds of rumors had been swirling around. Somewhere along the gossip grapevine, "medical leave" had leafed out into a nervous breakdown, which had become flipping out and being caught with a hydroponic grow-op (those crafty biology teachers), child pornography (all those computer babies, eh), or an arsenal of weapons and plans to wipe out downtown Hope Springs (those crazed Viet Nam vets are walking bombs). You could take your pick, or choose to believe he'd committed suicide over any combination of the above.

Sometimes, listening to another breathless explanation, Sam had been tempted to set the record straight, but then it had seemed to him that if you had to be notorious, it might as well be for something big. Take Sam's own case, for example. In hindsight, it was way better to have thrown up everywhere and passed out in the girls' washroom, than it would have been to, say, just puke in his locker. The first had briefly made him the legendary Chugger; the second would have made him Loser. Being run over by a scooter while flashing the library was no way to flame out.

And what would have been the point of defending Mr. Tegwar at school, anyway? Nobody would have listened. Sam had to admit that, in a sneaking way, he felt sorry for the guy. As usual, just why he felt this ambivalence was harder to pin down. Anyway, Mrs. Stephens had said that Mr. Tegwar wouldn't be charged with anything as long as he got treatment.

"Good," Sam's mom had said when he told his parents. "So he ends up with a broken ankle and the help he needs."

"Uh-huh," Mr. Foster's voice had sounded from beneath the kitchen sink, where he was tightening a loose connection. "They didn't tell us any of that at the staff meeting. Just said medical leave on a private matter and that he'd go from there to early retirement. Could you hand me the pliers, please?"

"Do you think he'll stick around town?" Sam had asked, staring into the toolbox. "What do they look like?"

"Sam, they're *pliers*, for crying out loud. That's what they look like. Could you hurry up? My back is killing me."

"Mm, I doubt it." Mrs. Foster had deftly extracted the pliers from a jumble of tools and placed them in Mr. Foster's grimy, outstretched hand. "Maybe it depends on how much this gets around. People in town talk, but they know how to do it quietly. And there are lots of things outsiders don't get told. But imagine walking around wondering who knew about you."

To Sam this sounded very much like being a teenager. From under the counter, a squeal of protest arose from something rusted.

Mrs. Foster went on. "On the other hand, where would he go? Back to the States? He's been here over thirty years."

"Well," Mr. Foster called, "there's some family there. He could. There was an amnesty, you know."

"An amnesty?" Sam had been all ears. "Wow. We all joked that he was like Rambo or something, but he really did war crimes?"

"War crimes?" His mother turned. "Honey, he was here because he was *against* the war. He couldn't get out of being drafted on religious grounds, so he came to Canada. There was even an anti-war group here in town that he was part of."

"Oh." Sam had processed this slowly: The bow-tied, clarinet playing, Rambo-fascist-homework-intimidation machine known as the Teginator had been a peace freak, a whaddayacallit ... a draft dodger. Probably this was no harder to accept than thinking of him as a library flasher. Or Mrs. Doberman as a MILF, drinking and smoking weed. Or a major-racked Mrs. Goldenrod bogarting. Still, it did feel as if the known universe had warped slightly. Into, dare he say it, immaturity.

"It's sad," Mrs. Foster went on. "He always seemed so fragile to me when he came in the store, all buttoned up and nervous."

"I know exactly what you mean," Mr. Foster had panted before the connection screeched again, "but maybe 'buttoned up' isn't the best way to put it."

"Ha ha."

"Let's just hope he's packed it in, as it were."

"Ha ha ha."

Sam ignored this. The Teginator as fragile—the universe *had* warped. Even odder, he had a feeling that he'd already known this. Was that why he felt sorry for him? Try telling that to the students at Hope Springs High. As a compromise he'd said, "Do you think I could say about the war stuff around school?"

"I suppose you could."

"Turn on the tap," Mr. Foster had called.

In the end, he hadn't. Well, he'd turned on the tap, showering his father with water, but he hadn't talked about Mr. Tegwar. (He couldn't think of him as the Teginator any more.) Something told him that the news would simply be woven into the rumors as more proof of the man's weirdness.

Now, out in the hall, Martha was hurrying his way, already holding her jacket. Sam assumed this meant she'd skipped last period again. She didn't have any books, either, and she had to have as much homework as him. For some reason this depressed him, too.

"Ready?"

"Well, I've gotta get my stuff."

"Hurry," Martha said.

He knew they had to finish the **Nicely Nautical** tonight. And, he assumed, find out what the Secret Weapon was. She'd never breathed a word about it and Sam couldn't ask because it would have meant admitting that he'd spied on her MSNing. Still, none of this would be until after dinner. He said, "What's the rush? We're not meeting till seven."

"I know," Martha said. "But no one's home at my place for a while."

Sam almost stopped breathing. He had the box of condoms in his backpack. And she knew that. Not to mention her online mention of the Pill. Did that mean ... Right now? Holy shit.

He didn't say that. Instead, inexplicably, he said, "I have to go to J. Earl's first."

Chapter Thirty-seven

It was a lie. What was he doing, Sam asked himself as they hustled toward Albert Street. Stalling, of course. But why? From the basement of his brain, a stream of hot thoughts of what they might do at Martha's was bubbling up. Except they were bumping into some definitely unsexy ones that had never popped up in any of the situations Sam had fantasized about, like, *How long before your mom comes home with the groceries?* and *Are you sure your sister is away?* and *I've never done this before and what if I'm not so good at it?* After all, look what had happened with driving. That was supposed to be easy, too. Did he want to do this right now? How could he be normal and *not* want to?

Because, hey, here was Martha, cute and funny, and hot—yes, definitely hot—and smart, and bold, and outrageous (today's T-shirt read HOLD MY PURSE WHILE I KISS YOUR BOYFRIEND); here was Martha practically saying, Let's go to my place and do it.

Or was he just plain wrong? Being wrong would be a hugely uncool Major Error. How could he find out? How could you ask somebody, even your girlfriend, *Do you mean we should go back to your place and have sex?* without sounding like a total idiot? Shouldn't he just know?

"See what I'm doing?" Martha said, beside him. She was panting a little as she tried to keep up with his strides.

"Huh?"

She was holding up a cigarette. Halfway to the filter a line had been marked on it.

"I'm cutting down," she said. "Now, when I want a cigarette, I only smoke half."

"What do you do with the other half?"

"Well, I save it. You know how expensive these things are?"

"Then why not just quit?" he asked, relieved to be talking about something else, even if this was a conversation they'd had before.

"Because it's *hard*, Sam. I never should have started, okay? I confess; I'm a criminal. Geez, give me some credit for trying. It's more than Lotus is doing."

Ah, yes, Lotus. And hswLarry. HSW. The uncertainty came back.

"Is your mom coming to the race tomorrow?"

"The Bitch?" Martha snorted. "Are you kidding? Now, if my dumbass sister was in a *tennis* tournament ... But my dad is coming for sure. You'll really like him."

And then they were at J. Earl's. Which meant that he had a whole new problem, since he actually had no reason to be there. "Wait here, okay?" he said to Martha. "That way he probably won't talk as much and it won't take long."

He hustled to the porch and rang the bell. What if no one was home? He shifted anxiously from foot to foot.

Mrs. Goodenough answered the door. "Sam! Surprise, surprise. What's up?" Mrs. Goodenough's voice had a way of carrying, partly because she directed plays for the Hope Springs Players, and partly because she often needed to drown out J. Earl. Sam glanced behind him. Martha didn't seem to have heard.

"I ... uh ... was just supposed to ask if J. Earl needed anything before next week."

"How about a personality transplant? Other than that ... but listen, if you've got a minute, what he could use is just a little visit from you."

"Really?"

"A little distraction wouldn't hurt right now."

"Oh. Well, okay, sure, I guess. For a minute."

"Good. Does your friend want to come in? Is she with you?"

"Oh, yeah. Well, no. Just a sec."

He ran back to Martha. "It's going to take a few minutes. I have to go in and everything. Why don't I just come to your place after—if there's time?"

"It's gonna take that long?"

"Well, I don't know. I hope not."

"Okay. But hurry." She looked at him and squeezed his hand, then flicked away her cigarette butt. It seemed to have been smoked past halfway.

"I will." He wondered if he was lying.

Chapter Thirty-eight

The Goodenough household had been restored to its usual order after J. Earl's bachelor week. The great man was in his office, a big-windowed room that looked out on the back garden. Shelves and a desk were crowded with books and an oddly high-tech flat-screen monitor. Between the windows, the walls were hung with framed newspaper cartoons of J. Earl, always drawn with an extra-large mouth, in the midst of various tempests he'd stirred up.

J. Earl was parked in the corner of a leather couch, staring out at the leafless yard. Sitting still, he seemed half his size. His face in repose was creased with lines Sam had never noticed. He looked at Sam.

"Foster." Not even an eyebrow twitched.

"I just came to see if you need any books for next week."

"Not a thing." J. Earl started a dismissive wave, then let his hand fall back into his lap. "I'm not going to any of it."

"You mean your week? How come?"

"Too tired, Foster; too old. Maybe it is time for a wrap-up on me, but I don't have to be there to see it."

"But I thought your leg was feeling better."

"Oh, my leg, my leg." J. Earl rubbed his face in his hands. "The hell with my leg. Marvell is wasting his time, you know. He wants me to be forty again and it's not going to happen. Christ, I don't even want to be forty again."

Sam could understand. Why anyone would want to be as old as

forty was beyond him. Although, if you were as old as J. Earl ... But the great man was continuing. "If Marvell put half the effort he puts into me into his own life, he might make something of it. You know, when he was deep into the drugs, he used to break arms for loan sharks? Has he shown you pictures of the 'house' he's building? It's a hole in the ground; a foundation with a tarp over it. And he says you can live in it. Sheesh. I think the only reason he does this physio business is because he thinks it's going to help him meet women."

"Maybe it will," Sam said. He was startled by this un-J. Earlish onslaught against Marvell. "Mrs. Doberman likes him."

"*Wha-at?*"

Sam started to tell what had happened at the committee meeting. As he did, J. Earl seemed to re-inflate.

"You've gotta be kidding," he said. "Hang on." He practically jumped up from the couch and, all but limp-free, swung the door to the office closed. "We'll keep this on the q.t. Siddown, siddown. Then what happened?"

Sam hesitated. He'd promised Martha to hurry and now J. Earl wanted him to take his time. He compromised by parking himself on the arm of a chair, then continued. When he finished, J. Earl cackled, "They're still at it. The smartest thing I ever did was to get away from those two. Thank God I met Dot again. I'll tell you, Foster, those women are the best reason I can think of for not being forty. I mean, there was a time when Goodenough was—"

"More than good enough," Sam finished for him. They were back on familiar ground.

"Damn straight. But the complications—whoo, boy."

"I know what you mean." Sam was beginning to think he did, too. "So, should we tell Marvell that Mrs. Doberman likes him?"

"I'm not sure 'likes' is the operative word." J. Earl's eyebrows were clearly in working order again. "Or if that's a blessing or a curse. Either way, let them handle it. They've both been around." He rubbed his hands. "Speaking of which, how are you making out with that little live wire who was with you last time? Still seeing her?"

"Martha? Oh. Yeah. I'm supposed to go there now." Sam rose.

"I like her. Spunky. She should lose the green hair, though." J. Earl opened the door again.

"It's pink right now," Sam said as he started through the living room. "We're supposed to be in the Leak race tomorrow."

J. Earl shuddered. "What the hell for?"

"I don't know," he confessed. "I don't really want to do it, but we've got a crazy craft for the 𝒩icely 𝒩aughty store—you know the one?"

"Oh, yes, I do ... heh heh heh. Hope Springs' hotbed of sin."

"Yeah. Martha and her friend say they have some kind of secret weapon for it."

"Dot!" called J. Earl, not listening. "Let's go for that walk and you can have a bloody cigarette."

At the front door, Mrs. Goodenough gave his arm a quick squeeze. "Super, Sam," she whispered. "I don't know how you do it, but you always seem to know the right thing to say."

He didn't even try to explain how wrong she was. At the end of the driveway, he looked at his watch. There was still time, if he headed for Martha's right now.

He waited for a car to pass, then turned for home.

Chapter Thirty-nine

The house was empty when he arrived. Good. He dumped his backpack on the kitchen table and slumped on a chair. Why was he hiding from a dream chance to have sex with Martha? It had to be what she'd meant. And what was he going to tell her? That J. Earl had kept him too long, he supposed. He almost wished J. Earl had kept him through tomorrow. Would she believe him? Why wouldn't she? But what if she didn't? J. Earl had groused about complications. When Martha got mad, boy ...

Or was being mad what Martha was really about? Was tomorrow going to be Lotus and Martha's big "up yours" to Hope Springs? They were always doing stuff just to piss people off. Martha was mad at everybody: her mom, her sister, *his* dad, Darryl, teachers, school.

That was crazy; Martha wasn't mad at him. And she wasn't mad at Mrs. Gernsbach. She wasn't even mad all the time; look at all the fun they had together. She wouldn't have been hinting that they should have sex if she was mad, right? Then why wasn't he racing over there right now?

Because he was a chicken, that was why. Like the guy in that love-song poem Mrs. Goldenrod had made them read, where he wonders if he can dare to eat a pear? Or was it a plum? Whatever. He groaned and rubbed his face the way J. Earl had, noting morosely that the three hairs on his cheek still didn't feel like five o'clock shadow.

Or was he being *mature* and *responsible*? Wasn't that what his mom would say? For sure, about going to Martha's—and she wasn't crazy about the Leak race, either. After all, even leaving Mrs. Gernsbach out of it, hadn't he done a world's record amount of looking idiotic already? Martha knew that. Was the Leak race idiotic or fun? Why was she making him do this? That was what it felt like: that she was *making* him do this, because if he didn't, he wouldn't be "out there" enough. And God knew he wouldn't be "out there" if he passed up a chance for sex. Well, yes, he would, but it would be "out there" as in shut out, instead of "out there" as in cool. And since they had protection, weren't they being mature?

Or was she *making* him do this, too? Why did the voice inside him keep chanting *Chicken* instead of *Bravo, O mature and responsible one*? Aaargh.

No, no, no, Martha wanted him. And if she wanted him, that was a compliment, right? But then, she and Lotus wanted Darryl for the Leak race and their MSNs said he was an idiot. And speaking of which, there were others for tomorrow; it wasn't like everything depended on him. So why did it feel as if it did? And what did the Leak race have to do with sex with Martha, anyway?

He groaned again. This was not progress. This was worse even than pre-Christmas. Geez, J. Earl had complained about complications when he'd done things; it felt to Sam as if the complications from *not* doing anything were even worse. It would be nice if he could shrink somehow and live inside his bass drum for a year or so, till things blew over. Imagining a miniature, trouble-free life, he leaned forward, closing his eyes, and rested his forehead against his backpack. It nudged a corner too uncomfortably sharp to be a textbook. The box of condoms. Oh, God. He went into the den and lay down on the couch.

A while later the phone rang. He let the answering machine pick up, then heard Martha's voice. He put a cushion over his head.

Mr. Foster came in a while later, toting several grocery bags. "Hey-ho," he said, looking in the doorway. "What's with you? Tired?"

"I'm not feeling so good," Sam said, truthful, if vague.

"You're not running a fever or anything, are you?" Putting down a grocery bag, Mr. Foster stepped in and laid an inquiring palm on Sam's forehead. "Nope. Well, take it easy; you've got a big weekend. Try to have a nap till supper time."

"Yeah." Sam sighed, hoping he looked drawn and pale.

Later, he guessed that he did have a nap because the next thing he knew, his mom was saying gently, "Sam, Darryl's here. Can you come and speak to him?"

Shedding the blanket someone had put over him, he stumbled, fuzzy-headed, to the front door. Darryl, fuzzy-headed in a different way, was shifting from foot to foot in the hallway. Now that nicer weather had arrived, he had paradoxically given up surfer shorts for jeans. "My statement has been made," he'd said cryptically the day he'd made the switch. The pants, however, were not what caught Sam's bleary eyes. Grinning from ear to ear, Darryl held up an object in each hand. "Sam, look."

In his right hand was a set of keys, in his left, a card. "I got it. I got my license."

"Wha-at? When?"

"Just now. My mom took me right after school. I didn't want to tell anybody so it would be a surprise."

You mean, so you wouldn't have to tell anybody if you failed, Sam thought uncharitably. But Darryl hadn't failed, had he? And now he was flashing an official Badge of Maturity. To Sam, getting his own driver's license seemed about as likely as Mr. Tegwar joining ADHD. His heart sank even lower. "Cool," he said.

"So, like, what time do you want me to pick you up? I'm allowed to drive to Larry's tonight."

"I don't know if I'm going." This was news to the rest of Sam's brain. Still, he rubbed his forehead, trying to look as if he was on the edge of something, preferably contagious.

"Why not? What's the matter with you, anyway?"

"I don't know, exactly. I was over at Goodenoughs' and I ate something and now I don't feel so good."

"Oh. Well, when will you know?"

"I'm not sure. Wait." Sam headed for the den, making sure to shuffle. He grabbed his backpack and returned to Darryl. "Here. You'd better take these, just in case."

He hauled the box of condoms out and handed them over. Darryl looked startled. Reflexively, he stuffed it under his hoodie, making himself look as if he was pregnant with a brick. "But you'll be there tomorrow, right?"

"Geez, I hope so. But I think I'd better rest tonight. I wouldn't want to—"

"No, you wouldn't want to," Darryl agreed. His eyes narrowed. "Hey, is there something better going on somewhere else?"

"No! I'm sick."

"Okay, okay. Call me if you're coming tonight."

"Yeah. Tell everybody I'm sorry if I can't."

Darryl the driver headed off. Sam headed back to the couch.

Chapter Forty

He skipped dinner. Thankfully, no one called so he didn't have to lie outright, and as long as he was doing homework, he could feel virtuous enough to ignore the inner voice telling him that he should call Martha. After all, he could still go tomorrow. Right? Wasn't he just being Mature and Responsible?

"How are you feeling?" Mrs. Foster asked around ten o'clock.

Sam shrugged noncommittally. He was lying on the couch, half-reading the assigned chapter in *Family: Transitional / Traditional*. The replacement for Mr. Tegwar had turned out to be even more of a demon for homework.

"Listen, I know it means a lot to you, hon, but maybe the race tomorrow is not such a good idea. If you're feeling sick, the last thing you should be doing is splashing around in a freezing river, especially with play practice, too."

Sam looked up, startled by this offer of a guilt-free excuse. He considered a token *Awww* of protest, then opted for a safer sigh. "Maybe. I'll see."

His mom's eyebrows lifted. "You must be feeling badly. Did I hear you say you ate something at Goodenoughs'?"

"I don't know if that was it." Keeping it this vague didn't count as an outright lie.

"Okay, hit the hay. I'll call you in the morning and we'll see how you feel. What time would you need to get up?"

"I don't know. Seven."

He didn't sleep well. Mainly, he was distracted by sex. If the once-every-six-minutes deal was true, he figured he was about two years ahead of schedule by morning. The only problem was, these were not sexy thoughts—they were worries. He'd thrown away the chance of a lifetime; he'd never get asked again. Was he really chicken? Did that mean he was impotent? Or did it mean he was gay? What if he couldn't ever do it?

And when he wasn't worrying about private sex, he was worrying about, well, public sex. He didn't want to float down the river in a pink wetsuit with a paper fig leaf glued on. He didn't want to see Lotus in fluffy red panties or throw condoms at little kids or get the town pissed off at Mrs. Gernsbach with a Secret Weapon. Could he keep on faking being sick? Did he still want to? Did he want to let everyone down? Finally, blearily, he decided to leave it all to his mom. If she got him up and thought he was okay, he'd go to the race. If not, he could truthfully say she hadn't let him. He closed his eyes.

After what felt like no more than a few moments, he opened them to the sound of footsteps in the hall. He closed his eyes again and rolled to face the wall. His heart began to pound. He heard the door open; another footstep. He willed himself to breathe regularly. A hand oh-so-gently touched his forehead. He shifted slightly. The hand was withdrawn. There was silence. Then a footstep, and the sound of the door softly closing. He opened his eyes. He was off the hook.

Chapter Forty-one

So why didn't it feel as if he was? Downstairs, he could hear the phone ringing, then his mom's voice in muffled answer. Would that be Darryl— make that Darryl the Driver—or Martha? His mom's voice stopped. He waited for her tread on the stairs. It didn't come.

His dad clumped down to the kitchen. Morning sounds filtered up to him. In a while, his mom headed off to the Bulging Bin. Some time later, he heard his dad go out, too. Through his window he could see that it was a beautiful spring day. That made it worse. He fell asleep.

It was getting on for noon when his dad came back home. By then, Sam was in the kitchen slumped over a bowl of cereal, wondering how he should contact Martha.

"Aha!" said Mr. Foster. "Feeling better?"

"Yeah," Sam said untruthfully, but wanting to get out of the house. "A lot."

"Excellent. You're back from the dead, and I'm just back from the river."

"How was it?" Sam asked, oh-so-casually.

"Oh, the usual gang of idiots. It always looks like fun if you're not in it."

"How was the *Nicely Naughty* boat?" Sam refined his question.

His dad shrugged. "Like all the others. It was pretty battered up by the time they got down river. Did you guys mean it to be like a giant bed frame?"

Sam nodded.

"Ah, I thought so. It was hard to tell. Some of that must have fallen off."

"What were they all wearing?"

"Pajamas. Over wet suits, I think; God, I hope. Carl Gernsbach had one, anyway." Mr. Foster laughed. "In fact, he was the best part. He had on this gigantic black corset thing, over an orange wet suit. It was a riot."

"Mr. Gernsbach! I didn't know he was going to be there." Was he the Secret Weapon? "Were they throwing the ... uh ... stuff?"

Mr. Foster laughed again. "Naw, they didn't throw anything. By the time they got down near the end, they had enough to do just keeping pointed in the right direction."

Sam had a sinking feeling of utter stupidity. He should have known the Secret Weapon would be a joke. He should have known getting down the river would be trouble enough; he'd done it before, hadn't he? He should have known the costumes would end up being pj's: Martha and Lotus weren't going to go around in sexy underwear. He'd over-reacted to the whole thing. Thank God nobody knew.

"Martha was asking for you," said Mr. Foster, pouring himself a glass of juice. "I told her you'd probably be revived in time for rehearsal this aft."

Sam jerked upright. He'd forgotten all about rehearsal. "Um ... how was she?"

"Wet," answered his dad.

"Was her dad there?" Sam described the man in the picture.

"Beats me; didn't see anyone like that. I was talking to her mom for a while, though. Nice lady."

Sam tried to phrase his next question carefully, then gave up. "Did she have a big argument with you at rehearsal?"

Mr. Foster drained his glass and put it in the sink. "I wouldn't call it an argument, exactly; more like a standoff. I wanted her to try something differently, to make it touching instead of comic, and she just refused. Face blanked like a curtain dropped. End of story. Get used to it. Which was irritating, but like I said, I've seen it before.

"And, hey, it's just a school musical. If she goes on, she'll have to learn some give and take, and a little trust, but that'll come. Say, you'd better eat more than that cereal. We're getting pizza in to rehearsal, but not until supper time."

Rehearsal was at two o'clock. They met Mr. Gernsbach in the parking lot.

"Sammy!" he called cheerily. "Where were you, man? We were cold but cool."

Inside, the stage had been set in the gym. Sam saw Martha in a cluster of kids on the first riser. Darryl was on the second, delivering what had to be a narration of the voyage down river. He swallowed, trying to look weary but recovering, and walked over, clutching his drumsticks.

"Hi," he said to Martha. Above him, Darryl's arms were windmilling, apparently indicating giant splashes drenching the **Nicely Nautical.**

Martha turned. Her face went blank.

Oh-oh, Sam thought. He pressed on. "Sorry about the race and, uh, everything. I just ..." He put a hand on his stomach. "At Goodenoughs' ... Darryl tell you?"

Martha blinked slowly. "Yeah. Then I met J. Earl Goofup and that big black dude in the hardware."

Sam felt his internal temperature drop. Martha went on, "He said I should be nice to you 'cause you made him a *surprise* visit and you couldn't be sick from eating at his house 'cause you didn't have anything. I said I already was nice to you. Screw that."

She walked away. When rehearsal was over, she left with Lotus and Larry. Lyle Doberman was waiting outside in his car.

Part Five

BRUSSELS SPROUT

Chapter Forty-two

Sam watched the last of the grade twos bounce out of the library, shepherded by some tired-looking teachers and parent volunteers. Behind him he knew Delft, Amanda, and Steve were slumped in chairs, recovering. Hope For J. Earl week was in full swing; the promised readings for school children had just ended.

"Nice going, you guys." Mrs. Stephens bustled into the meeting room. "Don't tell me they wore you out."

"If I ever have to do this again," Amanda said, "I want a whip and a chair."

It had been a long afternoon. Sam hadn't seen behavior like it since ... well, lunch at Hope Springs High. Partly, he knew, it was the way they'd read to everybody. Reading and showing the pictures at the same time was trickier than it looked.

On the other hand, *Louis the Loon*, J. Earl's contribution to Canadian picture books, was hardly a grabber. A story about an injured baby bird befriended by Painter Tom in Algonquin Park registered a solid ten on the Bore-o-Meter. How could a writer who was supposed to be so great ... well, never mind. This afternoon's efforts had left him only three hours from volunteer freedom. He did not feel liberated.

They ambled to the parking lot, still talking about how wild the kids had been. Sam kept quiet. Talking too much was a grade two problem. These days, his problem was the opposite. Martha hadn't said a word to him since that rehearsal after the Leak race, three days ago. Did this mean it was all over? Would they just never speak again? It felt more as if everything was hanging in the balance, like an overloaded cafeteria tray. So much for maturity. Sam felt as if he was back in grade two himself.

Amanda drove them back to school. She, too, had gotten her license after the driving course. As they climbed out, Delft said, "See you at practice."

Today was the last practice for *The Amazings* before tomorrow's dress rehearsal show for the grade sevens and eights from the junior high. The next day, Thursday, was opening night and the gala for J. Earl. Last bell was about to ring. Sam signed in and headed to the gym.

The place looked rather impressive. The stage was on three levels. The band's equipment was on the upper two: Sam and Mr. Gernsbach's on the highest, toward the wings; Darryl and Mr. Carnoostie's on the middle level, and closer to the center. Sam climbed up and seated himself behind the drum kit. It didn't offer any real protection from his problems, but he still felt safer.

A moment later, Darryl came in, munching popcorn. He offered the opened bag up to Sam. "How was the reading thing?"

"It sucked." Sam took some popcorn. "You seen Martha?"

"Uh-uh. You guys still not talking?"

Sam shook his head no. His mouth was full.

"Well." Darryl leaned in. His hair was almost normal again. "Larry told me Lotus said that Martha's got something planned for the show."

Sam swallowed. "What? No way." After all his worrying about the Secret Weapon for the Leak race, Sam wasn't falling for that again. Martha might be mad at him, but she wasn't going to make everyone else look stupid.

Darryl shrugged. "I dunno. Larry said that Lotus said that she had a big fight with her mom about something, too."

"So?" Now it was Sam's turn to shrug. "She fights with her mom all the time."

He wondered idly what she was reading. He'd started *Rule of the Bone* as soon as it came back to the library. It was no wonder she'd loved it. He missed talking about stuff like that.

More kids were coming in now. And there was Martha, wearing a T-shirt that read *Gentlemen, start your engines*. He watched as she strolled to the stage. A frown and her newly blonde curls made her look something like the actress in *The Maltese Falcon*. He realized that like Delft, she, too, was letting her hair grow. It looked great. How long had she been doing that? Why hadn't he noticed sooner and said something? Oh, God, why hadn't he gone back to her place? She was getting closer. Sam felt his stomach tighten. He tried to look good-humored and approachable. Martha ignored him and joined a group of actors. Sam bent and pretended to adjust his drum pedal.

By now, his dad and Mr. Carnoostie had arrived, with Mr. Gernsbach and his bass right behind.

"Okay, people," Mr. Foster announced. "We're only running the rough bits today; a few things still need smoothing out before tomorrow." He set a brisk pace as they ran through the parts. Sam was glad. He'd heard the music enough.

Finally his dad said, "Okay, last one, and it's a biggie: 'Brussels Sprouts, I've Got My Doubts.' It opens Act Two and we need a bigger ending. Dads, please."

Zack and Trevor took their places for the complaining duet. Zack now had a wide wicker garden basket to carry as a prop. His pants were as tight as ever.

"Right," said Mr. Foster. "We're going to try it with these." He dropped some tennis balls into the basket. "Instead of faking when you toss the vegetables in the last chorus," he instructed Zack, "I want you to really throw these over your shoulder. I'll have some plastic veg for you tomorrow. It'll add some energy and no one will expect it."

"Plus, it distracts from the singing," Mr. Gernsbach murmured. Only the musicians heard.

They ran the song. With Mr. Tegwar's clarinet missing, Darryl and Mr. Carnoostie were busier. The first two verses were straightforward. The singing was still bad but Zack kept his pants together. Then, in the last verse, he started heaving tennis balls. Darryl cried out. Mr. Gernsbach ducked. Sam, concentrating on an off-beat cymbal crash, looked up to see one zinging in straight between his eyes. He swerved and fell off his stool, taking the high hat down with him.

He struggled up, rubbing his knee. The high hat stand had clipped him on its way down. His elbow and rear end didn't feel any too good, either.

Mr. Gernsbach put down his bass and came over to help him up. "Good thing Scotty Tegwar isn't here," he called. "Imagine getting one of those up your horn."

There was laughter. Sam felt that a little more concern for himself would have been in order.

Instead, "Excellent," a grinning Mr. Foster enthused. "Now, we have to pace it."

He showed Zack which lines to throw on, then turned. "Okay, on that line, Brandon and Martha, you enter left and slowly move downstage, watching. You're stunned by what you see. Come to a stop just by Darryl there, and freeze, clutching each other. Zack, at the end, you hold up the last one, a Brussels sprout, so the audience can see it, *then* heave away."

"Zack, can you toss a little higher?" Mr. Carnoostie asked from behind the piano. "It's like a war zone back here."

"Yeah," said Sam, a little miffed that no one had even asked if he was okay.

"No, No!" Mr. Foster cried. "That's the point! It brings the band into the show. The fun part is, nobody knows what's going to happen. So whatever does, keep on going. Just this once, chaos is good."

"Then aim for Sam," Darryl put in helpfully. "He's the biggest target."

Off to the side, someone clapped.

Chapter Forty-three

The dress rehearsal next afternoon ended in wild applause from the grade sevens and eights. They hadn't gotten a single joke—except for the flying vegetables—but they had gotten the afternoon off to attend the show.

Mr. Foster gave everyone a pep talk about how much better opening night would be. The adults would get the jokes. Also, they'd be parents and family, and guaranteed to clap for anything. Mr. Foster didn't say that last part, but Sam had heard him mention it more than once at the supper table. Sam listened, standing near the back with Delft and Mr. Gernsbach. As Mr. Foster finished, Mr. Gernsbach grunted, "Gotta make my bus run, man. Good show. Hang loose."

The afternoon was almost over; the bell would ring soon. Sam sighed and joined Delft for the walk back to lockers. There was no point in looking for Martha. Despite the applause and the pep talk, he wasn't feeling so hot about the play right now, either.

"Oh, my God, I was so nervous," Delft said as they passed the office and started upstairs. "It was like being in Maple Nitro again."

"Really?" Sam was surprised. "You didn't look nervous. At least you don't get vegetables thrown at you." It had felt as if Zack were aiming at him. In fact, Zack had told him after that he had been taking Darryl's advice after all.

"Oh, but that's so funny!" Delft said.

"It's not funny, it's dumb. I'm scared he's going to hit me. Plus, it makes me look like an idiot." He didn't add, *which I already feel like all the time.*

"No. You looked … I don't know … flustered. But that's what's fun."

"Flustered is just as bad. At least you don't look flustered."

"Well, I feel it. But I'm acting, right? So you can't tell."

"But I'm not an actor. I'm the drummer and he's throwing stuff at me."

"Sa-am. Hello? The band is onstage, you're an actor. *Act* as if you're together. Remember when you drummed one-handed with the robot baby? That was so cool. God, we were all wondering what was going to happen if it cried, and you pulled it off."

"You still remember that?" Club Rockit and Baby Teggy seemed like a lifetime of failures ago.

"Of course I do," Delft said as they reached the landing. "It was great. C'mon." She tugged gently at his shirt sleeve. "You acted together then. You can do it now. Remember how nervous I was when I had to sing in front of Mr. Tegwar? You helped me then. Let's be a team. Like in the old band. Stick together?" Her eyebrows lifted hopefully, or so it seemed to Sam. Her face had gone pink, probably from the climb.

Sam felt a brief glow of satisfaction that Delft had remembered his moment of glory. Nice things like that were part of the reason he'd had a crush on her in grade nine. Plus, she had been remarkably hot in her country karaoke outfit. Teamwork, she'd said. Well, she was easy to team up with. But, act as if everything was cool? Was this different than *being* cool? He was a miserable failure at that. And what counted as acting cool in this situation? He'd figured out how to handle Baby Teggy. He hadn't been much good at figuring things out since. What was the—hah—mature response to being assaulted by plastic vegetables? Or to anything, for that matter? He had the depressing feeling that right now he was further from an answer than ever. He began to slouch.

From above, a voice called to them, "Sam! Delft!"

He looked up to see Mrs. Goldenrod coming down the stairs to them, waving what turned out to be that day's Hope Springs *Eternal*, the town's paper. She also had a new hairstyle that made her look like a very old teenager, and a tight-fitting red sweater that reminded Sam of that night at the library.

"Have you seen this? Isn't it great?"

She was not referring to her bust. Sam tore his eyes away. Mrs. Goldenrod was proffering a front-page picture of everyone at the library the day before, sitting amongst a grinning horde of grade twos. Delft and Amanda looked calm; Steve looked stoic. Sam, smiling idiotically, was sitting cross-legged with a pair of grade two fingers making antennae behind his head. At least his fly wasn't open. Or, wait ... Oh, God.

"This coverage is wonderful," Mrs. Goldenrod enthused. "Thank you both so much. Did you write down questions they had for J. Earl?"

Sam was still speechless with dismay. Delft nodded.

"Uh-huh. Mostly they wanted to know how he drew the pictures."

Mrs. Goldenrod frowned. "But he—oh, well, I'm sure he'll think of something. Or we'll make up some other questions, won't we? Anyway, I've got to run; the movies are tonight and then the journalism discussion." She started down the stairs. Over her shoulder she called, "I'm so sorry you won't be at the gala tomorrow—but good luck with the play. Break a leg!"

Sam watched Mrs. Goldenrod, or parts of her, bounce on down the stairs. "I don't think I'm cool enough to act cool," he sighed.

Delft said. "I bet you can. You just have to start somewhere."

Sam wished he had a map.

Chapter Forty-four

It was after supper when he finally picked up the phone; not that he hadn't thought about calling Martha before. At first he'd thought he should let her cool off a little, and then he'd thought that she would call him when she was ready; and after that, well, after that he'd been chicken because he knew he'd waited too long.

Now he punched in the number. His stomach clenched at the first ring, the way it used to when Baby Tegbun wailed. Another ring. Sam closed his eyes and tried to keep his mind empty. He'd decided to try not to worry about what to say, to just let something come out.

Someone picked up. "Hello?"

It was Martha's mom. Sam felt a jiggle of relief at this reprieve.

"Hi, Mrs. Sellers."

"Hi, Sam," she said. "You're turning into a stranger. I saw you in the paper today."

She sounded tired. He could hear music behind her. They chatted for a moment about tomorrow's show before she said, "You want Martha. I'll get her."

Sam heard the clunk of the receiver on something—the kitchen table, he guessed—then footsteps going away, and her voice from a distance. "Martha, phone! It's Sam."

Sam's stomach clenched again. The distant music did not have a calming effect. It sounded through the phone as if a radio tuner had slipped between reggae and rage metal stations. Which probably meant that Mrs. Sellers had music going in the living room and Martha had hers cranked in her bedroom. He wondered if Judy had ear plugs.

The rage metal ended and the reggae chugged on. Sam took a deep breath; Martha would be getting the upstairs extension. Nothing happened. Or had she picked it up but wasn't saying anything? "Hello?" he said. "Hello?"

More footsteps thudded, this time getting louder. His heart pounded almost in time. "Hello?" Sam tried again. There came a series of indistinct bangs and slams, cupboard doors maybe, then, away from the receiver, Mrs. Sellers' voice.

"Where are you going?"

"Out." It was Martha, but even further off. He imagined her by the kitchen door.

"Who with?"

"Lotus. What's it to you?"

"Well, don't forget it's a school night."

"So?"

"So don't be late, please."

"I'll be late if I want to. Don't be such a bitch."

"I'm not the one who's being bitchy. Could you at least hang up the phone?"

"Fuck you."

A door slammed. Sam hung up.

Chapter Forty-five

The air at Hope Springs High wasn't exactly crackling with excitement over the opening of *The Amazings*, but enough kids were involved to create a mosquito-sized buzz by Thursday afternoon. Everyone was under strict orders to be back at school by five o'clock to be ready for a seven o'clock curtain.

Mr. Foster opted to stay, but Sam headed home right at the bell. He was drained by a pop quiz on symbolism in *The Great Gatsby*. He would have thought Mrs. Goldenrod, who now had contact lenses to go with her hairstyle and wardrobe, had enough to do this week without marking papers, but no, apparently not. And he was fretting about Martha. He'd spotted her in the office again, notes and a textbook open in front of her.

Robin was at the kitchen table drinking coffee when he arrived. Sam grinned. He'd forgotten she was coming home for tonight.

"Hey, Rob."

Robin grinned back. She looked tired. She was wearing a high-necked jersey despite the spring weather. The cuffs hung down past her wrists.

"So ... " said Robin, as Sam helped himself to cookies. Sixteen years of experience told him she was building up to something, but he didn't go on full alert. The play and Martha had drained his defenses.

Robin took her time. Leaning back in her chair, she casually asked exactly the wrong question.

"How was the Leak race? Was the Nicely Nudie really wild?"

"Uh ... not exactly." Sam fumbled through a non-explanation that was supposed to keep everything vague. Partway in, he gave up and told her everything. Most of it, anyway. As he did, the phone rang in the other room. Unable to stop talking now that he was started, he let the machine get it, ending with his own call to Martha the night before.

Robin looked even more tired by the time he finished. "Man, oh man," she sighed, "is there anybody she isn't pissed off at?"

"Sure." Sam shrugged. "Lotus, Larry, I guess, Lyle Doberman ..." He thought some more. "Her dad. *He* never shows up and she's not mad at him."

"Well, she's pissed with you. No wonder. The not going to her place and then lying about it ... Oh, man, why didn't you talk to her, Sammy?"

"I've tried," Sam complained, deliberately misunderstanding.

"I mean *before*, idiot-brain. But wait, let me guess: You're a guy, and guys find it hard to talk."

"Yeah, I guess."

"Well, that is so lame. And it's bullshit. I personally have had it up to here with immature guys who don't talk." She sounded genuinely angry.

"Well, I was trying to be *mature*. Mom's always talking about 'be responsible,' so I was. Trying to be."

"Yeah, but you hurt Martha," Robin snapped, "and she really liked you. God, imagine how that would feel, taking a risk asking somebody like that and getting turned down *that way*? You don't want to have sex with her, fine. But just not talking to someone is not mature and responsible. Believe me."

"Sometimes it is," Sam protested. "Not saying stuff, I mean. That's the whole problem; sometimes it's mature and sometimes it isn't. How are you supposed to know? It keeps shifting around. It's not fair."

"What is this with you and 'mature,' anyway? You're always ragging on it."

Sam sighed. What was the point of hiding it anymore? Besides, Robin had just said she was fed up with guys who didn't talk. "Well, I guess I better tell you," he said. "Mom and Dad promised they wouldn't say, but I got in all this trouble before Christmas."

Robin leaned forward. "What'd you do?"

"Well, I found out Dad's computer password and, when they were out, I went on a bunch of ... uh ... porn sites, and then Mom checked Dad's sites to see if he'd looked at this garden stuff she wanted for Christmas ..."

"And you got caught. Oh, Sammy, big whoop. Everybody gets nailed doing that." Robin took a sip of coffee.

"Yeah, well ..." For a second Sam felt miffed that Robin was discounting his big confession. She didn't even know the sites he'd gone on. On the other hand, he had more to tell. "Anyway, while I was on there I saw this thing—"

"What kind of thing?"

"Never mind."

"Come on, Sammy. What kind of thing?"

"*Never mind.* Anyway, you could buy it and—"

"*What?* Don't tell me you ordered something off a porn site."

"Well, yeah. But it wasn't for me. See, it was going to be for this joke for Darryl."

"Yeah, right."

"*It was.* I was going to put it in his locker and—oh, skip it. Anyway, the thing is, you had to pay with a credit card, so—"

"Oh, Sammmm."

Sam swallowed and pushed on to the end.

"So I put it on the card Dad gave you a copy of and put it in your name—"

"*You what?*"

"I would've paid you back! I had the number from that time I had to order a train ticket for you. And I didn't think they'd notice. I mean, the company was called Erectable Industries or something. You wouldn't know."

"*Ewwww.* You would, too." Robin paused, then sat up straight and glared. "And let me guess, you used my address, too."

"Well, yeah. But, I'm pretty sure they canceled—"

Robin talked right over him. "Which explains the delivery notice that said I had a package from the States with twelve dollars customs and tax owing on it. *And* it explains why we kept getting those stupid gross catalogues. I thought somebody was pranking us."

"Us?"

"Never mind."

"Anyway, like I said, Mom checked Dad's sites and found out before they got the credit card bill and she was going to go ballistic, so I ... uh ... told her you did it. I said it must have been on that weekend you were home. But I forgot that on our computer all the log-ons are dated, so I got nailed for lying, too."

"Aw, Sam ..."

He looked everywhere but at Robin. "Anyway, I had to pay them back the money by working extra at the Bin—which I thought was totally unfair, because I figured they'd canceled the credit card charge—and I was supposed to behave better ever since, to show how mature I can be, and I just keep blowing it."

Now he looked at Robin. She was shaking her head. Was she also smirking? He felt vaguely insulted.

"Sam, you are such a bozo. God, do you owe me."

"Sorry, Rob."

"It's okay. I probably would have done the same to you a couple of years ago."

"You would?" Sam was shocked.

"Well, it would depend what the sites were and what you ordered."

Sam thought. "You would have."

"Hmm. Anyway," Robin leaned back, "so what are you going to do, break up?"

"I don't know. Maybe we have. It's not exactly up to me, is it?"

"Sam, what was I just saying? Sure it is; part of it."

"But she won't even talk to me! How do I know what she wants?"

"What do you want? That counts, too."

"*I don't know*. For everyone to be happy."

"Dream on." Robin gave a dry laugh and stood up. "At least you didn't get matching tattoos."

"No," he said, "Martha got a tattoo on her own."

"What, a tramp stamp?"

"No," Sam confessed, "I've never seen it. I guess I would have found out Friday afternoon."

"Oh." Robin enunciated the word with exaggerated clarity. "Yeah. Well. Sometimes the mystery is better than the enlightenment."

"Oh," Sam said, suddenly understanding something. "Grant?"

Robin rolled her eyes and nodded.

"Sorry."

"Thanks. I'll tell you later. At least they weren't his catalogues." She picked up her mug and turned to the sink. "Get the answering machine, okay?"

Sam went down the hall. The message was from J. Earl, who sounded excited. He needed Sam to "go somewhere" right away. This had to mean the library.

"Oh, crap!" He slumped. "What's this about? Doesn't he have to go to his thingy tonight? I've got the play at *five*. I have to be there."

"So?" Robin came up behind him. "It's, like, ten past three. You've got time. And when you go over, you can ask if I can have an interview with him—just a short one—tonight."

"What?"

Robin fixed him with a poker player's stare. "Do you or do you not owe me big time?"

"But—"

"This is going to make me look so good for work."

"But—"

"How gross was whatever you tried to have delivered to me?"

"Okay."

"Cool. You can come up and stay with me for a while in Toronto this summer. While you're there, you can even go to the delivery office and see if they still have *my* package."

"Cut it out. Can I really come up to Toronto?"

"Unexpectedly, I have extra room."

Chapter Forty-six

Sam scooped his mp3 player and hustled for the library. There were no books for J. Earl. As he stood, confused, Mrs. Stephens approached.

"Sam! Are you coming tonight?"

"I can't. I've got the school play."

"Ri-i-ight. I forgot. Break a leg. Anyway, I wanted to tell you, since you're almost finished volunteering, that we need to hire a couple of high school students to help with our summer reading program. If you're not sick of us, I think you should apply."

It struck Sam that he was being offered his first real summer job.

"Oh, wow. Cool. Thank you."

"Oh, no, thank you. You've done a good job here, Sam. Let me know by Monday."

Not knowing what else to do, Sam hustled to Goodenoughs'. He arrived, panting, at 3:47, by his watch, to find a massive baby-blue convertible parked, top down and gleaming, in J. Earl's driveway. It was Marvell's, Sam realized suddenly, stripped of its winter coat of aluminum foil. He stared, awestruck by its sheer size and gleaming detail, as he rang the front doorbell. Even the front bucket seats were two-toned—and oddly miniature-looking in their pre-headrest glory. It all almost made him want to drive again. Wow, he thought, things got weirder and weirder.

And weirder, when J. Earl answered the door. He was drunk. By now Sam could recognize the signs. Besides, the great man was holding a sizeable glass in which an olive lolled in some colorless liquid.

"Foster!" he cried. "Marvell, he's here. Let's go." J. Earl gestured at Sam with his glass. "C'mon in. I've just gotta whiz and grab supplies and we're outta here for the mystery tour. First, I'll finish my work-in-progress." He drained his glass.

"But—" said Sam. It was becoming his mantra.

J. Earl simultaneously pulled the door and turned, a move that caused him to stumble and fumble the glass. Then he steamed determinedly back into the house, bumping the kitchen door frame only slightly as he passed through.

Marvell appeared, looking larger than ever in his track suit.

"What does he mean, 'Let's go'?" Sam protested. "I can't go anywhere. It's ten to four. I've got the school play at five. It's opening night. I have to be on time."

Marvell nodded. "We've got a little problem here, Sam the Man. G's not in the best shape for his night, understand? He's been waiting on you; wants to show us something."

"Where? I've only got till, like—"

They were interrupted by the sound of a flush from the back of the house, then J. Earl's voice. "Any second," he called. This was followed by banging, clattering, and some surprisingly unimaginative swearing. Marvell sighed.

"It's news to me, too, bro. I don't know where he wants to go, but he's saying he won't do his thing tonight unless we take him. C'mon, man: We take the dude for a quick spin in my car, get him some fresh air, sober him up a little. No sweat. Hey, it's TDW."

"TDW?"

Marvell grinned. "Top Down Weather, baby, Top Down Weather."

J. Earl came weaving out of the kitchen. He was now wearing a tweed cap and a spring jacket, one pocket of which bulged. He looked pleased with himself. "Let's hit the bricks."

They trooped out to the car. Sam was surprised to see that the passenger side, till now hidden from view, was still primer painted in patches of gray and red. "How come this side isn't done?" he asked.

"Long story," said Marvell, now detailed in purple skullcap and wraparound shades. He eased behind the wheel. He was so big the low seat back seemed to stop just above his kidneys. "Short answer: a deficit in the pecuniary department. No green, baby. Climb in."

Sam got in the back. There were no shoulder belts, either, just lap ones. The monstrous car roared to life and Marvell slid them out of the drive. J. Earl gave directions. Heads turned as they rolled through town. Sam began to feel on display, sitting in the back seat. Darryl, he knew, would be doing a presidential wave or something. There not being enough leg room to slouch, Sam settled for looking at his watch: 4:05. He felt a twinge of nerves. Hope Springs High or Broadway, it was still opening night. Then something caught his eye. Part of a plastic bag was poking out on the carpeting from beneath the driver's seat. Folded-over lettering read: *Nicely Naughty*. To an all-too familiar reader like himself, it made perfect sense. Right now, he didn't care.

At the edge of town, Marvell gunned the engine and the car lunged like some kind of predator. Around them, the sun-washed landscape was beginning to bud. Sam got the full force of the chilly breeze. Up front, J. Earl said, "That's more like it," and reached into his pocket. "What's under the hood?"

"A three-ninety," said Marvell, then, "aww, G-man, that is un-cool." Sam scrooched forward. J. Earl was pouring more colorless liquid from a thermos bottle into its plastic lid.

"Strictly medicinal, Marvell. I'll drink; you drive." Sensing Sam at his shoulder, the great man said, "Martinis, Foster, made to my special recipe: All gin, and you wave a bottle of vermouth in the next room. Too bad you're too young." He set the thermos between his knees and screwed the top back on. Then he reached into his coat pocket and produced a bottle of olives. He handed it to Sam. "Here. Get one out for me."

Sam dutifully fished out an olive and dropped it in J. Earl's drink. "Cheers," said J. Earl. "You might as well hang on to those; I'm going to need them again. Next right, Marvell."

Sam sat back, holding the jar of olives and shivering slightly. The wind tugged at his hair. It occurred to him that after all the times he'd watched and read *Fear and Loathing in Las Vegas*, he was finally living a Gonzo journey across the countryside, with some minor differences: He was scared to drive; a senior citizen was doing all the indulging; and he had to be back in less than an hour. So vegetables could be thrown at him. It was depressing. He looked at the jar in his hand; he didn't even like olives.

Marvell made the turn onto a gravel road. Leaving a rooster-tail of dust behind, they passed several fields and came to a lane lined with bare trees. "Here," said J. Earl. He took a healthy swallow.

The lane dwindled to a rutted track that climbed a hill. Marvell stopped.

"I don't think so, G-man. That ground is going to be soft. We'll get stuck."

"We can walk from here." J. Earl drained the cup and unscrewed the thermos cap for a refill. "Where's my olives?"

With his drink in one hand and Marvell's supporting arm under the other, J. Earl led them uphill. The ground was indeed soft and slippery. Sam, fidgeting impatiently just behind, was still carrying the little jar of olives. It fit snugly in his palm, like a ball in a glove. His watch read 4:18. After all his recent mess-ups, he absolutely could not be late. "What happened here?" he asked as they reached the top, hoping to move things along. Since J. Earl was writing his memoirs, he figured this must be the scene of some past triumph. He hoped it wasn't a sexy one. That was so not on for him right now.

"Happened here?" J. Earl rumbled, still puffing from the climb. "Nothing yet. It's what it's going to ... be." He burped gently as he spoke. "Just look at this."

His drink hand swept across the vista. Marvell took off his shades and whistled. The hills of the county rolled in gentle tan waves, off in all directions. To the south, Sam could see the church steeples and two apartment buildings of Hope Springs, and beyond that the blue shimmer of Lake Ontario.

"Behold my next work-in-progress. A new chapter. Picture ..." J. Earl paused dramatically; or maybe he'd forgotten what he was going to say. Sam knew the feeling. In any event, the great man swayed slightly before continuing. "Picture a house, facing south. All windows, and the main room, up and out, like—like, uh, the bridge of a ship. Yeah. Aw, dammit, I gotta take another leak. Anybody here wanna trade prostates?"

He stumped to a patch of skeletal shrubs, put down his drink, and turned his back. "I'm about to piss in my dining room," he called over his shoulder. Then, "Maybe."

Sam took the moment to look at his watch: 4:22. With the ride back to town, a dash from Goodenoughs' to the high school ... He turned to Marvell and hissed, *"How long do you think this is going to take? I've got like ... I've got to go."*

Marvell turned up his hands. J. Earl rejoined them. "Wonderful, isn't it?" the great man said. "Saw this and I had to have it, no matter what. You gotta move forward, dammit, always forward, no matter what." He paused for a refill. "Olive."

Sam sighed and opened the jar. Impatiently he said, "If you're supposed to go forward, how come you're writing about all your past?"

J. Earl glared, then blinked suddenly, which spoiled the effect.

"I told you, Foster. Money. Cash. Moola. The long green. So I can *afford* to move forward. Now, olive."

Sam obliged, shaking the juice off his fingers. "Well, I have to move forward, too," he said. *"Please.* I have to get to—"

J. Earl wasn't listening.

"Anyway, except for Dot, you two are the first to see it. Cheers. It's happening no matter what the biopsy says." He drank.

Sam, tightening the cap on the olive jar, felt something tighten in him. Biopsy was a word he'd heard adults murmuring not long before his grandfather had died.

Marvell said, "Whoa, whoah, whoah. What's this biopsy? On what?"

"Nothing, nothing." J. Earl gestured vaguely with his glass. "I shoulda said test. On my tattoo. I'm right as rain." His cap had gone slightly askew. Sam looked over J. Earl at Marvell. Marvell cocked his head at the car. Sam, relieved, got the idea.

"This is really cool," he said, with a cheeriness not his own. "Thank you for showing us. But could we get back now? I have to get ready for the play."

"Works for me," said Marvell, equally cheery. "C'mon, G-man, we've got us some getting ready to do, too."

"So go," said J. Earl, looking off at the view. "Nobody's keeping you."

"And what are you gonna do? Walk?"

"That's the plan," J. Earl said with satisfaction. "With the help of my new hip and some liquid refreshment," he patted the thermos in his jacket pocket, "it ought to be a pleasant stroll. Good thing it's daylight savings."

"C'mon, man. That's got to be four miles."

"Exactly. And given the number of pit stops I'm going to have to make, it means I ought to get back to town too late for this wingding at the theater." He turned for the bushes again. "Speaking of which ..."

"What?" Marvell's voice hit a note Delft would have been proud of. "Don't be jiving with us, G-man."

"Nobody's jiving you, Marvell. And nobody's burying me before I'm dead, either."

"That is such bullshit!"

"No, it's not, Marvell. Tonight is bullshit! If it's all for me, then they should be happy if I do what I want, which is not to be there. Notice I didn't ..." another burp, "split that infinitive. Do you really think Felice Doberman gives a rat's ass about me? She just likes to run things, and schmooze the media types. And the only reason *they* want to be there is to ... to ... to ... stand in a spotlight. It's free pubicity."

Sam wondered what "pubicity" might mean. Marvell said, "Yeah, publicity for you." He fixed the older man with a heavy-lidded stare. Sam found it intimidating. J. Earl didn't; then again, his back was turned.

"Yeah, well, there'll be even more publicity if I blow off my own funeral, won't there? It'll be right in character for me, which is ... which is ... excuse me ..." Some unseen fumbling took place at his front, "... cantankerous."

"Mrs. Goldenrod cares," Sam pointed out. *Just get in the car*, he begged silently.

"Her circuits are fried, Foster. She was a sweet kid, but anyone who thinks my books are literary milestones needs therapy. I wrote her favorite book to buy a used car, for Chrissake."

By now J. Earl was bouncing oddly on his toes. "Aw, the hell with it." He threw up his hands in disgust and turned back to face them. Sam saw his fly was half open, jammed on the shirt tail that was sticking out of it.

"We care," said Marvell. "Dot cares."

J. Earl bent painfully for his drink. He rose, his face beet red, and stared back at Marvell from beneath his cockeyed cap. Then, very deliberately, he lifted the cup and took a long swallow.

"Suit yourself." Marvell snapped. He turned to Sam. "C'mon." He started down the hill.

Sam stood frozen, still idiotically clutching the olives. The clock was running. Marvell was already partway down the track. Sam looked back at the great man, who was staring resolutely, if a little blankly, into space, his shirt still poking out his fly.

A cry of pain wrenched the air behind him. He spun around. Marvell was writhing on the ground, just past a muddy smear on the soft earth. Sam dropped the olives and ran to help.

Chapter Forty-seven

Marvell was doubled up, clutching his right leg. "I slipped," he gasped. "It's the calf muscle. Can't tell ... if I tore it, or ... spasm." He grimaced as he rocked back and forth. "Help to the car ..."

"Okay." Sam knelt. "What do—"

"Help me up." Marvell clenched his teeth and rolled to his knees. He clamped onto Sam's shoulder and squeezed. It was Sam's turn to gasp. It was lucky he was already on his knees. He reached out to steady the bigger man.

A voice said, "Here, gimme your other hand."

Sam looked up to see J. Earl had made it to Marvell's other side.

"I ... oh, man ... all right, you steady, G?"

"Rock of ... Goldwater."

"All right, then. Help me ..." Marvell pursed his lips and pulled himself up. Sam felt as if he were being compacted. J. Earl staggered. "You got me? You gotta get me to the car. I need ... to get to ..."

"J-just take it easy," J. Earl stuttered with the effort of easing Marvell along. Sam could relate; the man's arm felt like a bag of cement. It occurred to him that a miniature drunken senior with a hip replacement was not the world's most reliable helper. If J. Earl went down, too ... He felt a twinge of panic. "We'll get you there," he said, with a confidence he didn't have at all.

They made it to the car.

"Can't drive, either," Marvell panted.

"Gimme the keys." J. Earl leaned against the convertible. His cap had come off somewhere. His entire head and neck were now flushed and he was wheezing in an alarming manner.

"Don't be a chump, G; you're juiced. Here." He pulled the keys out of his pocket and handed them to Sam. "Now, help me into the back. Easy ... *easy* ... *ahhh* ... I gotta try to ... G, get in the front there, I need my foot on your la—*ahhh*—that's it. All right, Sam, let's go."

Sam took a deep breath, got in the driver's side, and closed the door. The seat back felt as if it ended just above his boxers. On his right, Marvell's tree-trunk leg stretched across the console between the bucket seats and poked across J. Earl's knee. Sam reached to his left for a shoulder belt, then remembered. He fastened his lap belt, checked his mirrors, and turned the key. The car roared.

"Do the three-pointer," advised Marvell, ever the driving instructor.

Marvell's leg just missed the shift lever. Sam put the car in reverse. It was like turning an aircraft carrier, but then again, there were no curbs. He managed it, then eased them back along the lane to the main road. Even with his foot off the gas, the car urged itself forward like a racehorse.

They bumped up onto the road. Sam accelerated to twenty.

"Let's pick up the pace, Foster," came from J. Earl. Sam nodded and kept his eyes ahead. He gently pressed the accelerator and felt the power surge. Beneath the car, he could hear gravel clicking off the undercarriage. The steering wheel's rim was thinner and harder than the ones he was used to. He could feel a crack in it beneath his fingers. His hands began to sweat, but he held tighter and sped up to almost thirty.

From the back seat, Marvell called over the wind noise, "G, you got any o' that painkiller left?"

J. Earl fumbled back the thermos. "Thought you didn't anymore."

"I don't, but this is an emergency; I can handle it. Listen man, put your fingers behind my knee and down a little and rub my leg. Just gentle pressure, that's all it takes."

J. Earl began to probe Marvell's calf with what Sam could now recognize as the fixity of the truly bombed.

"Oh," gasped Marvell. "Ahh!"

Sam winced. He glanced in the rearview mirror.

"Ah!" said Marvell, "Oh, oh, ah!" Sam saw he was emptying the thermos over the side of the car as he groaned. He didn't have time to think about it; a pickup truck roared up out of nowhere, then whooshed past on the left.

"I thought you were picking up the pace," J. Earl growled. "You know the way to the hospital?"

Sam nodded. "You rub. I'll drive." He didn't even bother to wonder where *that* came from. Willing himself not to think, he stepped harder on the gas.

"Not the hospital," Marvell called. "G-man's place. It's easing a little, and if it is, one of your muscle relaxants oughta do it."

"You sure?" J. Earl twisted toward the back seat.

"Yeah, yeah; I'm cool." In the mirror, Sam saw Marvell close his eyes, a model of stoic suffering. "Just keep rubbing; that really helps. Oh, yeah, ohhh, yeah. And thanks for the drink, man."

When they pulled in, Mrs. Goodenough was on the front porch, a cigarette in one hand and a cordless phone in the other. She said something into the phone, stabbed the cigarette into an empty planter, and strode down the steps.

"Early, where the hell have you been? Look at you."

"Never mind," rasped J. Earl. "Marvell's hurt. There's been an accident."

"What'd you do, run into a gin truck? How many has he had, Marvell?"

"Never mind," J. Earl repeated. "We have to—"

"It's okay, G," Marvell interrupted. "That rubbing really helped. Sam can get me into the house. You go on in with Dot. Thanks, bro. Couldn'a done it without you." He carefully lifted his foot from J. Earl's lap. Mrs. Goodenough already had the passenger door open. J. Earl struggled to his feet.

"Thank God," he said. "I've gotta piss something fierce."

The Goodenoughs headed to the house. Marvell stood up. "You know," he said, "there isn't as much room back here as I thought."

Sam turned and stared. "Forgot to mention in my list of jobs," Marvell grinned. "I died in two movies. No Oscars, but I could take a fall." He stopped smiling. "Man, I knew he was edgy but I didn't know about this Big C scare. Well, we'll get him through tonight, first. But hey, bro, speaking of Oscars, very smooth on the play along. Formula One drive, too. Cool as a cucumber."

Sam realized his hands were still clamped to the steering wheel.

"Marvell," he said, "I was scared shitless."

"Never woulda known. Listen, man, you better split, you gonna make your play."

"OhmyGod," Sam froze. "What time is it?" He looked at his watch: 5:13. "I'm late. Oh, God, I am so late."

"So drive us to the high school, Leadfoot," said Marvell. "I'll drive back. Book your driver's test, too. You're ready."

He stepped over the console and squeezed into the passenger seat as Sam started the car again. "Speaking of making a play, my man," Marvell observed, levering the seat into its furthest-back position, "that Doberdude lady is not merely a fox. She is a cougar."

Chapter Forty-eight

Marvell took over the car at the front doors of Hope Springs High. He waved cheerily as Sam sprinted in. Sam raced upstairs to his locker, one-handed his combination, grabbed his drumsticks and the black clothes the band was supposed to wear, and hoofed it down to the gym. Mr. Gernsbach spotted him first. "Whoo, baby," he cackled, "the drummer who can't keep time."

"Where were you?" asked Darryl, who was fussing with his guitar tuner.

"Where *were* you?" asked his dad, who was fussing with everything.

"At J. Earl's," Sam said. "It was important. I'll tell you later." Or maybe he wouldn't, he thought, as he headed off to change. There was no reason to make J. Earl look dumb.

By the time he got back from warm-up in the music room, the premiere of *The Amazings* had an almost full house—or gym—ready and waiting. Sam tattooed a gentle beat on his thigh with the drumsticks as he peeked out from the wings. He recognized a lot of the audience. His mom was sitting with Darryl's family. A few rows closer, he saw Lyle Doberman with Lotus and Larry. They were, typically, snickering about something. He looked away quickly. On the other side of the gym, down near the front, he saw Mrs. Sellers and Judy. There was an empty seat beside her. He didn't see anyone who looked like Martha's dad.

Backstage, Mr. Foster called everyone together. They made a bizarre gathering in makeup and costumes. Delft was doing a little nervous shuffle Sam remembered from their Maple Nitro days. Martha was biting her lip. He wished he could tell Martha about J. Earl. He wished he could tell her everything. In fact, he wished he could tell her anything. He hadn't even noticed what her T-shirt had said today.

"Do you think she's gonna do anything?" Darryl whispered from beside him. Startled, Sam grimaced and shook his head no. He'd forgotten about that.

"Larry—" Darryl began, but Mr. Foster was calling for quiet.

"People," he said, "you have done a super job. You couldn't be more ready." This was not what Mr. Foster had been saying at supper last night, but Sam let it go. His dad went on, "Everybody out there thinks you're going to be good. But I know you're going to be spectacular. Don't rush. Keep it clear. Help each other. Enjoy it. It's a team effort."

A team effort. Sam looked at Delft. She looked back at him and gave him a tiny gung-ho smile. He looked at Martha. She didn't look back.

Mr. Foster looked at his watch. "Okay. Tech crew: out there and house lights. Musicians: after the audience settles."

Sam and the others lined up behind Mr. Carnoostie. The gym darkened. The murmuring of the audience stilled. Larry what, Sam wondered. There wasn't time to ask Darryl. Lights came up on stage.

"Let's go," whispered Mr. Carnoostie.

"Kick ass, man," whispered Mr. Gernsbach.

They filed out to polite applause and settled at their instruments. Mr. Carnoostie adjusted his score, then looked up at the others. He smiled. When everyone was ready, he counted them in. *The Amazings* was off and running.

Amazingly, it went well. The adults got all the jokes the grade eights hadn't. They also seemed to know when to applaud. It didn't hurt that they were big fans of the cast, either. Even so, Sam knew it was the best they'd ever performed. Maybe it was the audience, maybe they were just finally ready; whatever it was, the show was good. Not ADHD good, but good for a team effort on a creaky piece of schlock. Delft and her co-star declared their love for each other in a duet, and Act One ended to solid applause.

Everyone was bubbling at the break. Sam stood against the wall by the gym equipment room with Darryl and Mr. Gernsbach. Despite the good start and the satisfaction of just plain playing music, he was still feeling jittery. Partly, he knew, it was leftover nerves from his journey with J. Earl. There was a dark spot in the middle of his memory of all that—a word: Biopsy. Partly it was his troubles with Martha; he had to talk to her. And then there was "Brussels Sprouts, I've Got My Doubts." It was up next.

"Man," said Mr. Gernsbach, his gray ponytail bobbing above his black jersey, "back with the Ugly, this was when we'd step outside and smoke a fattie." Mr. Gernsbach was an old rock and roller. His first band, Buzzard Ugly, had been something of an underground legend as a cross-dressing precursor to punk music. Sam often wondered which had come first—the band's stage style or Mr. Gernsbach's own tastes. Darryl said, "Hey, you should have an Ugly reunion show to promote the store."

"You know, I said that to Delores, and she said only if we all went on diets first. Anyway, Tony's still in jail. I think. I should e-mail him and find out."

The conversation continued. Sam looked around. Where was Martha? Someone had dragged a couple of mats out of the equipment room, and people were sitting on them. He scanned the mats, flicked a glance into the equipment room, then down the hall to the change rooms, pretending he wasn't looking for Martha. He looked toward the stage. And there she was, in the wings, a little apart from everyone, peering out into the audience. She looked like the loneliest person in the world.

Here was his chance. His heart began to pound but he stepped toward her—and stumbled over an uneven join between two stage risers. Martha turned at the sound. Her despairing face went blank. She wheeled back to the audience and beckoned. The moment was gone.

Darryl came up beside him.

"I was trying to tell you earlier. I saw Larry and those guys out front. Think she's going to do something?"

Sam sighed.

"Nah, I saw them, too. Who cares? What's she gonna do, pull the fire alarm?"

"Five minutes to house lights, please," called Mr. Foster.

Darryl headed off to the washroom. Sam sighed again. It was almost time to look like an idiot. He glanced back into the equipment room. A box in one corner caught his eye. Sam came out of his slouch.

"Time, people," Mr. Foster called.

"What's that?" Darryl asked, returning.

"Padding for my stool."

"Good idea," Darryl said. "I've got a pain in my ass, too."

Various witty replies suggested themselves. Sam refrained.

Chapter Forty-nine

Onstage, he settled behind the drums and opened his score to "Brussels Sprouts." From behind the piano, Mr. Carnoostie looked to everyone, then nodded and counted them in. Sam hit the thundering roll that would bring the angry dads onstage.

On came Zack and Trevor. In costume, they looked exactly like teenagers dressed as grownups. Trevor was sporting a penciled-on moustache and a nasty-looking set of leaf clippers, Zack the basket filled with plastic missiles. They launched into the duet with gusto, if not much else. Clippers clicked, invisible crops were picked, and notes were dropped with abandon. And then, with thirty-two bars to go, right on cue, Zack produced a plastic green pepper. He heaved. Sam tensed. The pepper hit the backdrop curtain barely a foot off the stage. No. A fake cucumber arced over Mr. Carnoostie. He ducked. There was a ripple of laughter. Definitely no. A carrot nicked the bass amp. Closer. C'mon, Sam silently willed Zack. A potato zinged, high and well outside. Something told him to turn his head blankly, like a batter, and watch it go by. Darn. Still, there was more laughter. He played a tricky fill.

Now, on cue, Martha and Brandon began to move past Mr. Gernsbach. A plastic tomato hit the bass drum. Sam jumped, genuinely startled, but kept the beat. More laughter. He looked back to Brandon and Martha. They were approaching Darryl, turning for their look at each other. Brandon looked suitably horrified, Martha just grim. Given some of the notes Zack and Trevor were hitting—or not—this was understandable. Then, oddly, Martha took a slow step away from Brandon. She took another, still looking at him, turning her back to the audience. And another. Hey, Sam thought, what was—something sailed over his head. He ignored it. Martha was hooking her thumbs into the top of her long skirt, still backing toward the audience. A carrot sailed out into the crowd. Down front, he saw Lotus at the edge of the stage, with a digital camera. Sam suddenly grasped exactly where Martha's tattoo was and when everybody was going to see it. There was nothing he could ... the Brussels sprout finale was closing in. Martha was about to pass Darryl. Desperately, Sam smacked the ride cymbal on the wrong beat. Startled, Darryl glanced up from his chart. Sam flared his eyes in warning and jerked his head. Darryl looked at Martha.

Several things happened at once. Sam hit a tricky accent. Zack heaved the Brussels sprout. Darryl slid out a size fourteen sneaker. Martha tripped on it and went down as the Brussels sprout came sailing back, high and hard. Now, Sam knew. He dropped his left stick, slid his hand into the baseball glove on his lap, and stretched out his arm, still playing with one hand and his feet. The sprout smacked into the glove, an easy out in center field. He held the rubbery little replica aloft for a beat, then did a slow-motion topple off his stool, keeping the bass drum going as long as he could, and making sure to avoid the high hat. It still hurt but it didn't matter. The final bar was here. He raised himself from the floor enough to show his drumstick above the crash cymbal, one hand aloft in the lights, then smashed down on the last beat. The lights went out. There was an avalanche of applause. Thank you, Baby Teggy, he thought.

Chapter Fifty

"Ah, there's nothing like a standing o," Darryl said, as if his experience in the matter was vast. He had to raise his voice for Sam to hear him amid the post-show hubbub. High-fives were raining down like bonus points in a video game. "Naturally, we deserved it. Just wait till the next ADHD show."

Before Sam could reply, Zack was crying, "Sam! We've gotta practice that. I'll groove my throw!"

There were more high-fives all round. "The really cool throw was the one into the audience," Sam said, ensconced in a blissful cloud all his own. "That rocked."

"The whole thing rocked," said Mr. Gernsbach. "We had a definite groove."

"And we'll be even better tomorrow." Mr. Carnoostie came by. He paused to wipe his grinning face with a towel. "Delft," he called, "super show!"

"Yeah," called Sam. Everybody nodded.

Delft was with another group of kids. She held her opening-night flowers. "Hey, baseball star!" she called to Sam, and gave him a thumbs up. More congratulations were exchanged. Then, "What happened to Martha?" she asked. "Did she slip or something?"

Sam's blissful cloud evaporated. He looked at Darryl. Darryl looked at him.

"Uh, I don't know, exactly," he improvised. "There's a bit in front of

Darryl there where the risers don't quite fit together—"

"Yeah," Darryl put in, "one of the edges sticks up, like."

"—and I think maybe she caught her toe and tripped."

"Yeah, she did." Darryl nodded, and kept on nodding. "That's it, for sure."

The others moved on. "You *did* think she was going to, uh ... you know, right?" Darryl said.

Sam nodded reluctantly. "Yeah, I did."

"'Cause if you're wrong and she knows I tripped her, I'm dead meat."

"Tell me about it. *We're* dead meat. But listen ... um ... thanks."

Dead meat or not, it was a relief to confirm that Darryl had seen his signal and thought the same thing he had. He'd come through in the clutch. Darryl could be a good guy sometimes. He only hoped they'd been right about what Martha was up to.

"Hey, you guys!" Mr. Foster came up, beaming. "Great show. Nice playing, Darryl. And Sam, great bit on 'Brussels Sprouts.' I loved it; it made the number. Didn't I tell you it was better if the band was involved?" His brow wrinkled. "Say, what happened to Martha there?"

"She tripped."

"There's an edge where it fits together."

"Hmm. Well, she was way out of position, anyway. I hope she's okay. That was a bit of a tumble and she didn't seem to focus afterwards. Is she coming for dessert?" The Fosters and the Sweeneys were going downtown for an opening night celebration. Mr. Foster hadn't been taking in much about Sam's social life lately.

"She's gone already," Sam said. "She might have a family thing. Her mom and sister were here. She said her dad was coming."

"Really? I've never met him. Tomorrow, then. Are you guys ready? I've got a couple of things to do and then we're out of here. Mom and Darryl's parents are waiting."

Chapter Fifty-one

Sam drove his parents downtown behind the Sweeneys. Twilight had come on and evening chill was creeping out with the shadows. As they reached the traffic lights at the Four Corners, Mr. Foster commented on the unusual number of people who seemed to be out and about. "You'd better park here," he suggested to Sam. "I don't think there's anything free further down."

It wasn't until they were all walking to the Dreamboat Cafe that Mrs. Foster twigged to what was going on.

"Of course," she said. "It's the J. Earl celebration. I bet it's just getting out. See if you spot Robin. Maybe she can join us."

Sam scanned the crowd milling outside the theater. A TV crew had set up and lights were blazing. Several professional-looking photographers were snapping away. Looking further, he saw someone else.

Martha. Past the crowd, she was sitting alone on the park bench across from the library, smoking a cigarette. "I'll be right back," Sam said, and he started to run.

He got past the crowd and she saw him. Abruptly, she stood and took a step away.

"Martha!" he called.

She turned back at the sound of his voice. Her dark eyebrows pulled together and she sucked furiously on her cigarette.

All he could do was go for it.

"I'm sorry," he panted, pulling up in front of her. "I'm sorry I tanked on the Leak race, and the ... uh ... other stuff. I was chicken. I was wrong. I should've known it would just be funny and that you were being nice to me and I should've told you why. I was dumb."

She stared back, silent, over a wall of unhappiness. Into the silence he said, "We don't see things in the same way."

"Guess not," Martha said, and he could feel everything hanging in the balance. He tried not to breathe. Then, reflexively, she rubbed her arm, as if it was sore. Her wrist and the hand holding her cigarette had a reddish blotch, like a rash. Sam wondered if that was where she had hit the stage when Darryl tripped her. He didn't ask.

And then the balance tipped. She saw him looking and went blank. She rubbed her arm as if it was an act of defiance. And suddenly he knew he'd been right: She'd been going to wreck the whole play, everybody's work. Why? Just because of him? It didn't make sense. And now, did she know what he and Darryl had done? He felt empty. He wanted to say, *I know what you were going to do*, but what came out instead was, "I don't think we should go out together anymore."

The words hung between them, defying gravity. Martha's lower lip twitched almost imperceptibly. Then she said, "Like I care. I'm out of here." She spun away. Without looking for traffic, she started across the street.

"Can we still ..." Sam called after her, but the words sounded so lame, that he couldn't finish the *be friends* part. He already knew the answer.

Martha made a half-wave without turning. Whatever. A car pulled up in front of the library, bass speakers throbbing. Lyle Doberman was at the wheel; Sam could see Larry and Lotus inside. Martha flicked her cigarette away. Her friends were waiting.

Chapter Fifty-two

Sam walked back toward the theater. He had the leaden sense that now, finally, he'd totally blown it—worse than Baby Teggy, worse than throwing up at the dance, worse than the spring break mess, or even driving up the hydro pole. This time he'd hurt someone else more than himself. And this time there was no way to make it right; no volunteer hours to atone with; nothing he could scrub clean; no tattoo to hide. It was something small and dark and dense inside him that was his to carry from now on.

The streetlights were on; so was the theater marquee. In bold letters it proclaimed: HOPE FOR J. EARL. Sam felt a stab of memory. Was there hope for J. Earl? A biopsy, he'd said. That was a test for cancer. Yet, up ahead, the great man was smiling and posing for photos in the glare of TV lights. Had Marvell and Mrs. Goodenough worked magic? How could you maybe be dying and do that? Which would be worse, knowing or not knowing?

Knots of people were beginning to drift his way, heading for cars and home. One figure limped alone. With a start of recognition, Sam called, "Mr. Tegwar!"

His old teacher looked up. Sam ran over. Mr. Tegwar was wearing a jacket and tie Sam recognized, but his collar hung looser and his jacket seemed baggy. Had he lost weight, or did he just deflate somehow, away from school? Mr. Tegwar's eyes flicked nervously behind his glasses. Then he pursed his lips and lifted his chin in the old way, standing his ground. Sam realized that now that he was over here, he didn't know what he wanted to say. It occurred to him at the same moment that he might not be someone Mr. Tegwar wanted to run into. After all, Sam had been one of the first on the scene the night things had gone so badly wrong at the library.

If that was the case, Mr. Tegwar didn't let on. He gave a clipped nod. "Hello, Sam."

"Uh ... hi, sir."

"I've just been attending the festivities for Mr. Goodenough, who I knew some years ago. I believe you know him, too. It was too bad you didn't a-attend; it was quite enjoyable."

"Yes, sir. I wanted to," Sam lied. "But it was opening night for *The Amazings* at school."

Sam saw Mr. Tegwar almost flinch, but turn the motion instead into an effort at standing even straighter. "Yes, of course. I sh-should have remembered. I trust it went well."

"Pretty well," Sam said. Then he found himself adding. "But we sure could have used your clarinet."

"Really." In the gray evening light, Sam saw Mr. Tegwar redden a little. For a second, his lips seemed to wrestle with a smile. "Well, I'm sorry I couldn't play."

"Oh, that's okay," Sam shrugged and immediately felt like an idiot for doing it. "Anyway ... uh ... I should go, but I just wanted to say I'm ... uh ... sorry you're not at school anymore. It isn't the same."

Now Mr. Tegwar did smile. "Thank you very much." He extended his hand. Sam shook it. He wasn't sure where what he'd said had come from, but it felt like the right place. And it wasn't a lie.

He was standing a little straighter himself as he came up to Robin. She was looking professional, with a notebook and pocket recorder in her hand.

"Who are those guys?" he asked, not really interested. A group of oldsters was posing with J. Earl.

"Heavies," snapped Robin. "Pierre Farley, Munro Atwood-Munro, Stephanie Leacock, and Margaret Connor Richler. Don't you know anybody?"

They watched as chipper smiles were recorded. Sam noticed J. Earl had steered them to pose in front of the display window for *Nicely Naughty*.

"Did you ask about my interview?" Robin reminded.

"Not yet."

"Sam!"

"There wasn't time. Stuff happened." Sam slouched again. Another failure.

Another picture was taken. "Okay, thanks, Earl," one of the photographers said. Apparently the celebrity quotient had been exhausted. The TV crew began to turn its lights away to film its reporter.

"Listen," J. Earl called to the photographers, "will you just get one more for me? Dot!" he called. "Where's Dot?" The great man looked around. "Marvell!" he called. "Felice! Elvira! I need all my spark plugs." Then, "Foster! Didn't see you there; get in here."

Startled, Sam stepped forward. Mrs. Doberman and Mrs. Goldenrod stuttered up from opposite sides, making too-modest *who, me?* gestures. Marvell and Mrs. Goodenough materialized. J. Earl looked at Sam and Marvell.

"Who'd'a thunk it?" he said. "You boys clean up real nice."

Sam remembered he was still in his black dress pants and shirt. Marvell wore an elegant black suit with an ease that proclaimed past acquaintance with the good life. His limp had cleared up nicely.

They huddled close in front of *Nicely Naughty*, Sam and Marvell anchoring either end with their height. Mrs. Doberman, in a yummy-mummy gold dress, stood next to Marvell. Mrs. Goldenrod was beside Sam. The Goodenoughs took the middle. Mrs. Goodenough brushed something from her husband's shiny head.

The photographers shuffled. As the lights came back on, Sam couldn't help but notice the snug fit of Mrs. Goldenrod's dress over her bust. Something sparkly in the fabric really caught your attention, and what was underneath kept it there. It reminded him of the sweatshirt with the squinty lady on the chest, which reminded him of all the slogans on Martha's T-shirts, and he stopped staring as he felt the dark weight settle inside him again, right over his heart. Though, come to think of it, he felt a weight *outside* him, too, right over his heart. Curious, he reached into his shirt pocket and found the Brussels sprout.

"What the hell is that?" J. Earl turned at his motion. "No upstaging."

"It's a fake Brussels sprout," Sam said, handing it over.

J. Earl gave the object an inquiring squeeze. "It's not fake. It's real. You've gotta start eating your vegetables." His lip curled. "What a nasty little growth," he murmured. Then, "Goddamitt," said J. Earl, "I'm with you. I hate this stuff."

He leaned back and tossed it into the air. The sprout bounced off the combed-over pate of Munro Atwood-Munro, who was blathering into Robin's tape recorder.

"Oww!" The icon looked around angrily.

"There," said J. Earl triumphantly, "there's a little acting-up for your memoirs, Foster. There's a use for everything." He snugged an arm around his wife's waist and pulled her close. "Now, everybody think about sex."

Marvell smiled suavely. Mrs. Doberman giggled. Glancing back, Sam saw Marvell's hand on her shapely, gold-covered backside. Sam shook off his slouch. He stood up straight and smiled. He didn't much feel like smiling yet, but that was okay. Sooner or later he would, maybe after he asked for Robin's interview and drove everybody home. In the meantime, nobody needed to know the difference. If Mr. Tegwar and J. Earl could do it, so could he.

"Closer," said the photographer. Everyone shuffled. Mrs. Doberman giggled again. Beyond the lights, from the twilit edge of the onlookers, there came a smaller flash. Sam hoped it wasn't Mr. Tegwar. Straining to see, he spotted others instead: Mrs. Stephens, Smitty, his parents, the Sweeneys. Darryl was talking to Amanda. Mr. and Mrs. Gernsbach were rounding the corner. And just ahead of them was someone else: Delft. She, too, was on the sidewalk, her parents chatting to someone behind her. Delft, though, was looking at him. Now she saw him looking back and she smiled, waving a tiny wave, her hand at her waist. It was a great smile. He found himself smiling back. A real smile.

All at once, he knew he was in the wrong place. Delft's parents were speaking to her. They were starting to move. It was now or never. As he broke from the pose, Sam had a camera-flash thought that he'd be no more than a blur in the photo, a question mark. That was okay; he didn't know any answers, either. For now, he had a feeling it was okay to be a work-in-progress.

INTERVIEW

with

TED STAUNTON

What was your inspiration in writing about the life of Sam Foster? Is it your memory of being that age yourself, or your observation of teenagers today?

Two things led me to write about Sam in this book. First, I'd written about him in two previous books (*Sounding Off*, and *Hope Springs A Leak*) and I wanted to know what was going to happen to him next. Second, my son Will and his friends were having an interesting year in grade eleven and I thought, how can I let all this good material go to waste? I didn't have to make this all up, you understand.

My own experience of high school was way different: I was handsome, wildly popular, brilliant, athletic, played guitar like Hendrix, dated five hot girls simultaneously and was the entire student government. And that was only grade nine. I also have a bridge in Brooklyn you might want to buy.

In the course of this story, Sam trips up in various ways that call into question his ability to become "mature." In fact, his mistakes and miscalculations end with the worst failure of all: hurting someone he cares about. That makes the book seem sad, though not exactly tragic. Could you comment on that?

I think that Sam, typically, has it a bit backwards. (Can things be *a bit* backwards? Hmm.) Anyway, it seems to me maturity comes from reflecting on the times we mess up and learning to accept responsibility for what we do, even when it hurts. That means the messing up is an integral part of the process: unless you've actually been tested or tempted by a bad choice it's all theoretical and easy.

So, when Sam messes up with Martha, it's a terrible lesson he has to learn. Because that sadness stays with him he grows from the mistake. And you have to cut him some slack; keep in mind that there is no way he's ready to deal with someone as troubled as Martha is. Not even *Martha* is ready to deal with Martha yet. In fact, she seems to me the more interesting question. Sam hurts Martha for sure, and she has huge issues. She also hurts a lot of people. Is she ready to think about the consequences of her behavior to friends, family, and at school? Just because she seems more adventurous doesn't mean she's more mature. Messing up may be integral, but remember, the maturity comes from reflecting on it.

What's the origin of the humor for you? Is humor in fact all about point of view? (To Charlie Chaplin's little tramp, the pratfall isn't funny.)

Absolutely. I think humor is all about point of view. (I don't imagine it would be that hard to change *Hamlet* into a dark comedy.) The point of view for humor has to be that of an outsider. Someone who's in the game has too much at stake to find things funny, but someone who feels excluded often makes up for it by mocking whatever they are left out of. I think it was Mark Twain who said that you had to be angry about things to make them funny, and maybe he's right. I think you can just outgrow them or still feel some affection for the things you joke about. After all, someone else said we only tease people we like.

This is essentially a comic novel, but Sam's girlfriend Martha is a poignant character—angry and needy—and in the end a rather sad figure. What place did she have in your thinking about this story?

In terms of storytelling, some unfunny bits give breathing space and make the funny bits sharper, just like funny bits in a scary story give you a break from the suspense.

More to the point though, if you want to write about something close to real life, you have to put in the unhappy bits too. There are a lot of Marthas out there, no matter what their name or gender. They have a tough time, and make life tough for people around them. Sam is a pretty stable, decent guy. He's going to make it. It's important to remember that it isn't like that for everybody.

In this novel, as well as in others you've written about the town of Hope Springs, a number of adult characters appear who are more than just background. In some fiction for teens, adult characters are only sketched in, but in _Acting Up_, J. Earl, Marvell Byrd, Mr. Tegwar and others are more rounded characters. How does the story gain by the inclusion of these people in Sam's world?

I don't know that the story does gain. It does for me, but if you are fifteen it might bore your butt off. I hope readers let me know. When I was a teen, adults were another species entirely, but an intriguing one. (Now that I am theoretically an adult, everyone is a mystery. This is why I write stories. At least in a story I can figure somebody out.) I guess I'm hoping some readers will be as curious as I am. Oddly enough, life is full of everyone, and no matter what most teen movies and fiction imply, you can't exist in an adult-free world, particularly if you need meals and rides. Know your enemy, it's often said. Well, suck it up, teens, it won't be long before you *are* the enemy.

In this book and its predecessor about Sam, *Sounding Off*, music plays a big part in the story. Is it important to you, too?

I'm glad you asked me that. My dad was a musician, music is huge for me, and my son is trying to make it his career. If I hadn't ended up doing this, I would have tried harder to be a pro musician, instead of a part-timer like I am today—not that I would have been great at it, or anything. Writing is deferred gratification: "maybe someone will read this someday;" music is instant. One of the fairly cool things about this Internet age is that an adventurous listener can explore "old" music as easily as cutting edge stuff, which means that I can sometimes listen forward and my son, say, can listen backward. Then we can share—or tell each other how wrong we both are. It's great.

Since his 1983 debut with *Puddleman*, one of Canada's most perennially popular picture books, Ted Staunton has been entertaining readers of all ages with his funny and perceptive stories of youth and family life. His many other books include the novel *Hope Springs a Leak*, which was shortlisted for both the Ontario Silver Birch and Nova Scotia Hackmatack awards, and its sequel, *Sounding Off*, also set in the fictional town of Hope Springs.